SPACE ADVENTURE

How To Time Travel Between Planets

By Phoenix Armstrong

INTRODUCTION

I want to thank you and congratulate you for buying the book, *"Space Adventure: How to time Travel Between Planets"*.

This book contains proven steps and strategies on how to be imaginative.

This book will make you attach yourself to the protagonist. His journey, though occurring in different planets and galaxies, will make you feel that in every one's life—a hero's journey is a must. Every human, no matter how strong, or how fragile, have to continue their journey with persistence.

Thanks again for buying this book, I hope you enjoy it!

© **Copyright 2020 by Phoenix Armstrong**

All rights reserved.

This document is geared towards providing exact and reliable information with regards to the topic and issue covered. The publication is sold with the idea that the publisher is not required to render accounting, officially permitted, or otherwise, qualified services. If advice is necessary, legal or professional, a practiced individual in the profession should be ordered.

From a Declaration of Principles which was accepted and approved equally by a Committee of the American Bar Association and a Committee of Publishers and Associations.

In no way is it legal to reproduce, duplicate, or transmit any part of this document in either electronic means or in printed format. Recording of this publication is strictly prohibited and any storage of this document is not allowed unless with written permission from the publisher. All rights reserved.

The information provided herein is stated to be truthful and consistent, in that any liability, in terms of inattention or otherwise, by any usage or abuse of any policies, processes, or directions contained within is the solitary and utter responsibility of the recipient reader. Under no circumstances will any legal responsibility or blame be held against the publisher for any reparation, damages, or monetary loss due to the information herein, either directly or indirectly.

Respective authors own all copyrights not held by the publisher. The information herein is offered for informational purposes solely, and is universal as so. The presentation of the information is without contract or any type of guarantee assurance. The trademarks that are used are without any consent, and the publication of the trademark is without permission or backing by the trademark owner. All trademarks and brands within this book are for clarifying purposes only and are the owned by the owners themselves, not affiliated with this document.

TABLE OF CONTENTS

The Hidden Treasure 1
Unexpected Can Anytime Loom In 25
That Thing! 31
The Magician 37
Knowing The Truth 64
Cruel Fate 69
The Dragon's Belly 72
Two Tough Fates Meeting 87
The Ultimatum 99
Conclusion 108

THE HIDDEN TREASURE

It was unexpected that it would be snowing in the planet of Oasis, formerly known as Jupiter. There were also less crafts because of the demand of the noble people living there. They wanted to adapt the mannerisms of Earth—the appetite of rich—mainly of the people that belonged to the twentieth century. This was what Clark was thinking too. His hidden aircraft entering the planet and the exposure of his emotions going high and low looking at the sceneries below, he felt ready. The surge up of his emotions was sometimes high because he was excited; sometimes low because he knew the people below weren't noble. They hid under their posh appearances, neglected that their bodies were not part-human and part-robotic. But Clark knew the reason for this wintery weather. Last year, one of their agents kidnapped a citizen of Earth who had found a way to change the weather of any planet. He was living in New York City, his presence captivated by the tallest skyscraper. Dr. Hamilton was getting the different definition of being a famous person. He was an innovator, but he stayed at his apartment under the plain mannerisms of the people who suggest a sense of threat to them. He was still lying in the bed, trying to wake up. The government had locked him down. They had told him that his presence was ubiquitous among other planets. Their people had eyes on him, 'and it was just a matter of day...' —he never completed that sentence in his mind. His round face was like of the innocent man, but his lush hair on top was the result of his instant transplantation—it tried to give him the look of a younger man. At first, he felt proud of it. He thought that ambition and looks made him. But soon, he didn't like the peculiar difference of his older body matching the fresh strands of his hair.

Dr. Hamilton was under the impression that even though he was old, but his body would age like a fine wine. He had taken laser-telomeres injections: to replace his old body cells, so that new body cells could make his body to function like a 20-year-old. His was one-hundred-twenty. That age was the peak point of his life. He had learned that how the practical actions, not just thinking, could change the world. For the last eighty years, he was working on the weather, to change it, so that he could change the world. Well, he had achieved his dream, yet this paradigm shift, it brought him not just success, but also the attention of lousy bureaucrats residing all over the solar system. He started getting invites to visit their planet. He had become a celebrity, but it was in the eyes of the common people. In the eyes of the government, he was just a tool. His invites were just the impractical places—a trap, to caught him, and to declare to the different worlds that he was dead, but it was a way for the different bureaucrats of different planets to use his talents, to make him a puppet by hiding him.

His first invitation was to the planet of Zam, formerly known as Saturn. He was scheduled to arrive at one of the asteroid belts around it. He was excited. He was confident and arriving at the palace, he felt a great sense of relief. The expanse of Zam filled his sense with amazement. Though he had visited the planet virtually, and sometimes, holographically, but with the presence of his soul, the big ball of the planet made him awe in wonder. He told himself not to get excited, when it was the time to be serious; he told himself he had to be focused, when he felt that his awareness was spreading all over the luminosity of Zam—both the belts and the planet. He took a breath before the podium, and before the audience that wore shawls—light emanating from it, giving them the peculiar distinction. This code of dress was new to him, yet he thought that it was perfect for his night of grandeur triumph. The fire inside his heart ignited the flame of vision—a kind of flame which the growing men hoped, but could not able to accomplish because the short-term gratification gets them: they want results too fast. But Dr. Hamilton, he knew that fast results didn't produce longevity; it was like a drug that gave pleasure at first, and hell in the end. He understood the meaning of exponential growth: striving to achieve a vision made him what he was today, and its manifestation was the scientists in front of the podium, sitting and looking up at him. Well, this moment of bliss was all just for a minute. These elements got changed into a new theme when people started appearing one by one right next to each row where the scientists of Zam were sitting. They all appeared to be wearing a mask. Their dress was all black. From their arms shined an armor that produced a light which seemed to faint all the gathered scientists of Zam. For Dr. Hamilton, there was no time to think to come with any kind of explanation. His jolly face got turned into a creased forehead, and if he hadn't done the instant-transplantation, the old gray hair of his would have experienced goosebumps.

His head was instantly gazing like a bird all around the room, giving every sign of strain to him. Then suddenly, a man—his dress all black, just like the people standing at each row—teleported in front of him. Dr. Hamilton leaned back and put ahead his right hand as a sign of protection. He couldn't make out what was happening. The sudden flash of light from that same man was blinding him. The rays were coming from his eyes. It was making his world to spin as his eyes were stunning him by the power of its mockery, and he couldn't do a damn thing about it. The mild trembling of his voice: "What are you…doing…to…me?" were the last thing he had remembered. His world shifting and tilting, he wasn't aware when his consciousness left him.

Dr. Hamilton thought that he died, but he woke up in New York City, in the most luxurious skyscraper. He was struck by wonder that he was in an apartment, its number 849. The windows around him and his bed in the middle was giving him the view of flying cars getting past him. The neon lights in the sky amalgamating with the pink, it was the reflection of different corporations around him. Whether some had the vibe of partying, or whether some had the vibe of meeting—he couldn't tell. As a matter of fact, he did not care. The only thing he wanted to find out was that why he was there—why was he in New York City?

He flickered the blanket over his body to find out that. He felt pain getting up. Somehow reaching the bathroom, he looked at the mirror. The sudden flash of light coming from his eyes gave his body a shudder. For a moment, he thought that he was in a dream, but when he again glanced at the mirror and when his face reflected back, he could see that his natural eyes were gone. His new robotic eyes—it gave the natural feel, but the yellow lights were new. It was like an in-built torch that he was carrying. Shock was dissolving inside his brain slowly. The sense perception of reality was telling him that he wasn't dreaming, and that everything was real. Realizing that, the floating gestures of his hands were slowly approaching his face. Upon touching it, he realized that that the area below left jaw line, reaching up to the area below his lips, and ending up at his chin, was all metal. The moment he touched it, the moment it was that the shade of his color got changed and was replaced with the actual robotic shine. Standing all naked, not only one-third part of his face was in steel-color, but that color also covered his left arm, and the lower-abdominal part of his body. Anger clogging up in his body, making his face red, he slammed his left hand on the mirror. The glasses were turned into smithereens, and Dr. Hamilton was amazed.

Deep inside, he felt a relief that he had become strong. It was like an unadmitted emotion, but he also couldn't get the reason of his lower back pain. As he turned to have a glance at it, he couldn't conceive the reality of this situation. There was circuitry installed in it, only the charging wires were lacking. He immediately hurried to the room, to his bed. He completely took out the blanket and over it he found the wires. He felt like the bureaucrats had caught him into a vicious trap; he wasn't aware how all this would unfold his life now. Coming over the bed, Dr. Hamilton held the wires in his hand. He also heard the ring of a bell. Completely ignoring it, he proceeded to plug those wires into his lower back. He immediately got a shock. His body lying flat on the bed, as if sleep had stabbed him from behind, he convulsed, then again, the lights of his world went out.

He woke up to a lullaby: "Hush, little doctor, don't even utter a word. I'm gonna buy you yours life time worth. If you won't corporate, I have to operate. I think I forgot…you see what am I doing here?" Clark's voice was slowly registering in his mind. The view of the world around his eyes came back slowly; it came with the shifts and tilts. This time the pain at his back hurt him bad. As Dr. Hamilton raised his hand to touch his back, Clark halted him. The shifts and tilts under his eyes were setting under the natural order of habitat. He still couldn't make out the face though but could see the cheerful confidence that Clark carried. He didn't know why his lips were tightened. To that, he gave Clark a silent stare. Somewhere in the deep part of his mind, he was thinking about his past: how he non-stop worked to achieve the shifting patterns of weather; now, he was thinking that the result of his vision was some kind of torture that he had to endure. He didn't feel strange that Clark was sitting next to him in his bed. The bone structure of his face was in symmetry, he could see that. His eye brows were dark, he could see that. He had a decent head of hair, he could see that too.

To him, Clark seemed like a nice guy, but suffering inside him provided him the urge to compare the two of them. He was still looking at Clark, thinking.

"Are you gonna say something?" asked Clark.

"Who are you?"

"I'm the guy that saved you."

"I don't get you."

"Can you see those robotic parts of yours?" said Clark.

"Did you give me those!?" Dr. Hamilton got up furiously from his bed. The yellow light under his eyes became dark. The posture of his body had turned erect, like of the warrior, not like the stature of any scientists. He was surprised looking at his new avatar. He didn't feel the sense of being a doctor. The energy inside his body felt new. Clark conveyed that the man who had kidnapped him was a secret spy working for the people of Oasis. They had sent him along with the rest of his gang. After capturing Dr. Hamilton, they had kind of dismembered his body, Clark had told him that, while also saying to him that they were planning to steal his mind; they were planning to turn him into a puppet robot, where that body would be like a slave. The mechanisms of easy manipulation in that body worked at its best and the exploitation in that body would also make someone reach that level of physical torture where choosing death was a better option.

"How did you free me?" asked Dr. Hamilton.

"I knew a thing or two about his eyes," Clark answered.

His tone of causality made Dr. Hamilton to think that behind his good-looks, there was a thoughtful face. "I didn't catch your name," he said.

"It's Clark Hemmingway."

"So, Mr. Hemmingway, what did you do to me?"

"I assembled you. With the kind of material that I have attached in your body, that man will never make you sleep again."

"So, why are you here?" spoke Dr. Hamilton.

"See, Hem. Can I call you Hem? Looking at your expressions, I think I can. So, Hem, the reason I'm here, to simply put, is for your protection."

"I don't need protection."

"They can still dismember you. The government told me to captivate you. The parts in your body are still fragile. Just like normal body needs rest, robotic body needs to rest too. What I mean is…just charge yourself, Hem. They can come here at any time—the people who harmed you. They can still harm you. If you don't recharge your body, and if they come, it is just a matter of day…or seconds…"

Clark assured him he didn't need to worry because when he told him that and didn't complete his sentence, Dr. Hamilton had worn a glance of stress. In actuality, he felt like he had lost his way. It brought back his sense of threat, that fear of death. And another theory which stated that the government had locked him down. He thought that his mental stage of life had come to a point where some spiritual practice was required. He felt like Clark was the guy to whom his practice of spirituality would shine. He could feel the serenity under the presence of his aura, which made him conclude that Clark could be a consistent meditator. Thinking that, he didn't feel vulnerable any longer. But suddenly looking at his delighted gestures changing into a look of bewilderment, it made him cautious of the environment around him. Dr. Hamilton immediately looked at his back. The cars that were flying past his skyscraper were froze as if the time there had been stopped. When he, in an instant, returned his glance at Clark, his body got froze too. Everything around Dr. Hamilton felt alien. He couldn't able to breathe properly. His head started aching. The severity of it was too bold that he held his hands around it as if wrapping it to stop the pain. But the pain didn't stop, so does the sense of normal time around him. He again thought that he was in a dream, but when the same people started emerging at his room in a random position—all wearing black, their face hidden with a mask, their arms shining an armor, everything jolted him. It again brought him back the fear of death.

Ahead of him, a black portal was forming. He felt like the world was suspended there. When a man appeared from it wearing the same clothes like of the people around him, Dr. Hamilton's brain associated him as the same man that had dismembered him—a spy that had been sent from Oasis. He could see his glowing eyes—this time the color of it was sharp, as if the actual sun was looking at him, again with that same mocking manner. He thought that he was going to die, when he saw him; he thought that he would be badly hurt, when he saw that man's hand approaching his shoulder.

"Relax," he spoke with his heavy voice. The people around him had sunk to their knees. Dr. Hamilton couldn't speak even if he wanted to. The man had the movement of dereference when he walked up to Clark, leaving the doctor. Clark, even though his body was paused, he could still see him. He could see Dark Storm in front of him—the name that gets tossed on around the different galaxies like a vicious tale to feel frightened, he was looking at that actual man acknowledging him. Nobody had ever seen Dark Storm taking out his mask, but as he was looking at Clark, he was revealing his face. When he was doing that, all his members that were on their knees had hit their face with their shining armor that was attached to their arms. Dr. Hamilton, as he witnessed this current event, he didn't know what to do. He could see the whole room glowing—the kind of light rays that he couldn't take. It was coming out from the eyes of Dark Storm. The whole room had become too sharp that it was like the color of sun that was spreading, like dark matter spreads in every universe. Before fainting, again, unable to believe, and watching the fading environment around his eyes, he saw Dark Storm burning Clark's eyes, while his figure stool still, not able to do anything.

Clark was thinking about the same incident when his feet were under his silent aircraft. After got hit with the rays of Dark Storm, the government had pronounced him dead. But the secret service people took him to examine his body. They were surprised to find out that his body structure was made of Ferus-Steel—an adamantine formation, like of the rock but was harder to corrode by any chemicals in any universe. Though the masculine structure had the will to be brought back to life, but the eyes, they were hollow, and some kind of ash seemed to be submerged there. The hollowness had affected the brain. Clark was kept in a capsule for more than five years. The scientists that worked for the secret service, everyday they saw him. They watched that Clark's bone structure, it was helping other parts of his body to heal faster. The flow of his blood was gradually coming to normal. Keeping his heart pumping with the capsule pod, while his brain dead, for scientists, this all was an experimentation. But astonishment struck them when they saw remaining cells of his brain rejuvenating, coming together, trying to give Clark a life. When he woke up, he was recovering fast. The pod has given him all the necessary abilities, which he was lacking, that his body required.

After touching life again, the only mission he had in his mind was to find Dark Storm. Only few members of the government knew about him, including the members of secret service. Major Kyle had warmed him about Dark Storm, also telling him that the earth was in allied with Oasis. If he had planned to do anything to them, he might put earth in jeopardy because the ways of Oasis were non-forgiving and it was the most dangerous planet in the whole solar system. But witnessing everything from the above, he could see spires like of the twentieth century. The most hottest planet had the shower of snow on it. Clark concluded that it was the result of Dr. Hamilton's weather discovery. The so-called noble people, their persona part-human, part-robotic—mostly the mechanic part of their body outweighing the normal body parts—they brought Dr. Hamilton just to wear more clothes to hide their robotic parts, so that they could appear outwardly more human, but inside more enhanced. Clark couldn't get this illusion. He came alone in the planet of Oasis, against every warming that the secret service members of the government gave him. As far as Dark Storm was concerned, he had told himself that he mustn't permit himself to feel anything. His anger was like a string that was pulling himself to take immediate actions, but a different part of his mind was speaking to remind himself that he needed to hide in the frankness of people who were tyrant, so when chance comes, he would definitely stab them in the back.

Below him was a castle. Its spires were imitating the universities of the twentieth century. When he jumped from his silent aircraft, he had the parachute on. In the mid-air, his parachute vaporized. The holographic 3d technology couldn't help him; it was struck with a distortion by an unknown transmission, cutting the actual algorithms run by his silent aircraft above. Coming at a tilt, his velocity as if of an asteroid, he straight away headed to the upper section of the castle. Just below one of the spires, he hit a mirror with his head, then immediately touched down the red carper with a roll and got up. He was amazed to see that he was in a hallway. Seeing people having a dinner under a long table, the lavish white table cloth, over it the dripping candles, and people having the glass of wine—whatever they had planned for the day and had expected, everything went completely dark when they saw Clark. Their positions were paused like a statue, unable to believe what they were seeing.

"Como estas usted?" spoke Clark. They could see that he was real. "No, espagnole?" then he said to evoke their discovered amazement.

The most so-called noble man, the one sitting in the biggest chair, he could see that his people were lost somewhere. To direct them, he shouted, "Get him!"

"Did I do something wrong?" asked Clark; then he looked behind the shattered mirror, the cold hitting his back. He could see that the man who was directing the meeting, directing this dinner, directing this night—his people, they were late to take the moral action that was required to take Clark down. His buffed body, exposing the kind of hairy chest that would make any girl's heart pound, his white shirt rolled up, and the thread of his hair moving with the frigid wind—the noble man directing the castle, he could spot the eloquent essence of his universe: a bright confidence, a young blood, his purpose sharp, and he all prepared. Clark, when he saw the noble man's eyes, that it had started to glow, he became vigilant. The people coming his way, their eyes too had started to turn the same way. If their illumination could be compared to the glow of Dark Storm that his eyes emitted, it was nothing. The first person that confronted Clark came with a sword. The grip he had on the lightening sword was faster than anything that Clark had seen in any imitating historical epoch. That man had planned to cut him in half, but that sword did nothing. Clark's rigid bone structure, after spending more than five years in a capsule pod, had made his body to endure most of the vicious atrocities coming at his way—he just found out that the swinging sword was one of them. When he realized that the sword did nothing, he smiled at the man. His punched him so hard that his body leapt a few feet away and was met by a wall. His face was all shattered. The people around him, they all had the look of panic when that happened. To that, they all started teleporting inside the hallway.

The main so-called noble man was still. He understood that his people had broken a law. Teleporting was only allowed when they had to travel to another solar system, or another planet. But inside the realm of Oasis, that wasn't allowed; of course, following the twentieth century model was tough, but observing Clark was tougher than anything he had seen. Clark couldn't get who was appearing suddenly in front of him, lashing his lighted weapons and disappearing. This constant teleported attack, though it did nothing to his body, but it agitated him. To counter that, he thought about jumping to the long table, where all the so-called noble men were having dinner. When he did, he was smashing their food; some were still sitting on the chair, terror-stricken; especially, some women, who Clark had smeared their face with their food. He could see that people weren't coming at him on the table. To them, having their footprints on the table was considered a bad omen. The main noble man, sitting on the biggest chair, he was preparing to launch himself into an explanation in order to buy some time, in order to halt Clark's abstract mannerisms, which he was seeing in the form of reality.

As Clark was coming near him, he teleported himself, then in a second, he came back again. The arched door behind him got opened. There were two beautiful women who appeared to walk at Clark's direction. He was still on the table, standing. He was amused, at the same time, felt strange glancing at those women. They were slender-looking, had long hairs that were cascading down their back. To him, they looked delicate, while they walked naked. He had forgotten what course of action he had to take if they try to do something to him. When they came near him, they paused. Their breasts were aimed at him. He thought that the noble man was presenting him a course of pleasure to leave him and his people alone, but when a strange scent from their nipples got released, a fog formed around him. It made him faint and his body got dropped on the table, while breaking it.

When his senses came back, he was in a cave bound by bars. He immediately got up and made his way release himself by breaking the bars, but all he got was a shock that made his body bounced a few feet away. Though the electric shock didn't hurt him, but he was trying to crack the formula that this castle had. He didn't have any clue. Clark felt like he sometimes had to put aside his pride—to not look at the world as an easy instrument to claim what he desired at any time. A part of his mind was saying to him that he should have listened to Major Kyle, another part of his mind was reminding him about his incident with Dark Storm. Somehow breaking into his ship and rescuing Dr. Hamilton had made him believe that the virtue of his life had the kind of power that had the power to break any resistances. But he was proved wrong when Dark Storm burned his eyes. He had seen him in the ship soaking up some kind of energy from a portal that was situated behind his throne. When he was taking up the energies, he was vulnerable. Dark Storm couldn't able to defeat Clark, but when he came to confront him, he had this unsurmountable power that killed Clark. He was an honest man who had been swallowed by the dark itself. And now, in this cave, under the dark, alive again, he felt lost. Then he heard a voice: "Are you just gonna look ahead of you?"

"Hem!" Clark responded. His voice came like an assurance and for Dr. Hamilton, Clark's presence provided the same to him. He could see that over the years Clark had become sharp, his agility like of a child who wanted to fix everything at once, whereas, Clark could see that Dr. Hamilton had become fat, the sharpness of his body had been lost. On top of that, the robotic parts of his structure had been removed. His instant-transplanted hair was gone too. He had been surviving on a pill, he had told Clark that for the last seven years. Even adding that Dark Storm had delivered him to the main ruler of Oasis, Alfred Cox. The ruler had demanded Dr. Hamilton to change the hot weather forever. He gave him five years to study the weather of Oasis. Coming from an educated background, but held by a regime—in the eyes of the people, a government—Dr. Hamilton had to obey him. Other choice was the puppet slave which Dr. Hamilton had to avoid at all cost. After changing the weather, Alfred had allowed him to live as a free man in the planet of Oasis, not in any other planet, and with a different identity because in the eyes of the people residing in different solar systems Dr. Hamilton was found dead at his apartment number 849 in New York.

Living in Oasis, visiting different regions, he had become sick of gothic structures, which all the time had been covered up with snow. He also wasn't allowed to altar his body: to replace it with any machine parts, which the people of Oasis did often, used the weather as an excuse to hide their robotic parts with different clothes. This silly thing was like a vision of malice to him. Though he was a free man, for some time, he felt like he was bound by chains, mainly psychological. Even the new strength that he had received and realized at that night in New York, before fading against Dark Storm burning Clark's eyes, his new body of strength—on Earth, it seemed stronger, but on Oasis, it proved futile. Every human being he met, he saw that each one of them was stronger than him; in few cases, where he thought that he outweighed that particular person's strength, he eventually found out that person had the power of teleportation. This power was only used under the mandatory situations where one's life was in jeopardy, and in fact, this power of teleportation had been used on Dr. Hamilton.

In those few cases, he somehow escaped that power of someone hitting him unknowingly from an unknown place, but he felt that if he kept on picking up someone, his safety on Oasis would become a compromise. He had conceived that reality, but he didn't know that reality would come true. Upon receiving five years to study the weather, Dr. Hamilton was able to change the weather within four months. After being released as a free man to only roam inside the realm of Oasis, also being confronted with their people, he got to know to that he could also achieve the power of teleportation. The only problem was that it was in the region of Yanturi where Alfred's castle was there. It was located in the south, whereas, he was in the west. Couldn't find any feasible mode of transportation: airplanes only allowed for few of the noblest man, and for rest of them, a car, it took him time to reach Yanturi. It was always the place of celebration; news of conquering planets by diplomacy, or sheer power always spread around the town. It gave the people of Oasis a marvelous confidence—a pride of brainless hatred. He even got to know about Dark Storm, that he not only conquered planets, but he belonged to a different dimension—a dimension that had no name. In other galaxies, his name was also associated with antimatter. His close association with Oasis, it concluded other planets to think that Dark Storm was born there. This allegiance added an extra weight—a massive difficulty for different democratic planets to end the regime in Oasis.

Even after coming to Yanturi, Dr. Hamilton had witnessed a massacre where a subordinating Dark Storm ship was destroying a factory. The gigantic aircraft had covered the nuclear factory with an invisible fence. The people that were running out of the factory couldn't able to break the fence. They were trapped. They couldn't do anything when the beam of light from the aircraft had hit the factory they were working in. The different beams of lights striking everything under the fence had turned the factory into ashes, along with the people that were running from there. Dr. Hamilton didn't feel anything, neither resistance nor regret, neither any kind of emotional pain, or suffering. His body equipped with few robotic parts, he had started to feel less emotions. Though the fear of death scared him, but he had to use the faculty of his logic to move ahead in life. He knew that every world had its two coins: good and bad. He just had to get far way from the bad. But reaching to Yanturi, he saw that the castle stood on the peak of a mountain, white with marbles, different structures around it with onion shaped domes—all small compared to the castle in between. The spire of the castle emitted a purple light. It was like magic to him. He knew that it was the room in the spire where the power of teleportation was kept. Dr. Hamilton was going there. He knew that he was going toward the bad according to his intentions, but he told himself that he had to take a risk.

That risk had landed himself to the jail of Vroxtal. The jail was situated in the north. The ruler of that region was Isaac Holms—the noble man who had called the two women and, from their poisonous gas, had made Clark faint. He was listening to Dr. Hamilton's story. He couldn't reach the verdict how he exactly ended up in the jail. To him, it seemed like Dr. Hamilton was skipping an important moment in his story.

"Did you reach the castle? Were you able to reach the purple spire?" asked Clark.

"I was. Entering the land of that castle, I was met by this girl who claimed to be Alfred's sister. Her name was Elizabeth. She told me the way to access that purple portal where the power of teleportation resides. She had told me to meet in one of the attics. She gave me this chit. But I didn't see her. Instead of her, guards came out. They arrested me. And I was sent here. I'm living here for the past seven years. What happened to you?"

"I'm alive," replied Clark.

The mild contradiction of his cheeks told Dr. Hamilton that Clark now had a strong past—to solve those atrocities, he needed the future as a vengeance. He could see that Clark was paying attention to the guards outside, their bodies teleporting constantly. This flickering motion of soul, he thought that if he could have this power, he would solve the world. Looking at them, he demanded their voluntary cooperation, even if they were enemies, even if he was trapped. This idea made him to punch Dr. Hamilton, to see that whether his strength lived with him, or not. Even though after the capture his robotic parts were removed, but when Clark punched him, his eyes glowed with range, as if something that was lost had come back. He then pushed Clark—at least, tried to do. His body built like a rock; it was heavy; it didn't move. It produced a hard-hitting sound. Their fighting—for Clark, a show, for Dr. Hamilton, a rage, it brought attention. The guards constantly teleporting, one of them came inside the jail, Clark held his body, and in a moment, that guard had done his teleportation, allowing Clark to come out of the jail too. The moment he was out, he punched the guard, making him sleep forever. He also had broken the chain of the flickering movement of their transportation: no more guards were coming. He had halted their movement. Taking the key out of the guard's pocket, he made Dr. Hamilton free.

"I was here since seven years, and you just took me out of the jail…just like that?"

"Yes, Hem. Just like that. Universe is like silence; it needs two things to make ten thousand things, and then to millions, then trillions. What I mean is, a bond requires two particles. Since seven years, you were single. When I came, we created a bond. And sorry," spoke Clark.

There was blood coming out from the side corner of Dr. Hamilton's lips. To that, he chuckled and wiped his trailing blood with a left thumb. In order to safely get out of the castle, Dr. Hamilton had to wore the guard's clothes. As far as Clark was concerned, he had to find a guard to match his body structure. All the guards they had seen stealthily, they had found one guard who matched with the height of Clark, only different was that he carried a huge gut with him. And the other problem was that he was standing on the rampart, near its entrance. Coming from the jail to the top was easy. But over the outwardly appearance of the castle, guards lingered everywhere on different ramparts. The hallway through which Clark and Dr. Hamilton was passing, the next point was where the guard was standing. He was showing its back. His tall figure reaching almost the top, this made Dr. Hamilton conclude that Clark was maybe six feet four inches tall.

As their footsteps started reaching near him, the guards ears began to twitch. As he looked back, he saw Dr. Hamilton as a guard having his lighted sword over Clark's neck. Seeing Clark on his knees, he was shocked. He had met him in the royal dinner, filling everybody with disgust and torment. But on his knees, it brought admire in his eyes for Dr. Hamilton.

"Are you okay…" —he was trying to remember his name— "…mister?" he then said.

"I'm fine," replied Dr. Hamilton. "My is name is Hem by the way. All I need is your assistance."

At first, afraid, then seeing Dr. Hamilton's eyes like of a boastful man, he started to walk. The moment he came near Clark, he was met with a low blow. Lights from his eyes got immediately shut and his body collapsed making a heavy noise.

"You don't have to kick him in the nuts," spoke Dr. Hamilton.

"Hem, we don't have enough time."

"We do have enough time. What are you planning to do?"

"We are going to Yanturi. I need that power of teleportation, that hidden treasure in the purple spire. I need to defeat Dark Storm. But first, I need to defeat Alfred."

"Are you crazy?"

"All heroes are crazy until they prove their worth. And besides, don't you wanna leave?"

"What about your ship?"

"It wasn't mine. It was from my government. They don't trust me that much."

"They never do," replied Dr. Hamilton.

Wearing the clothes of that guard, Clark and Dr. Hamilton went down the castle. The kind of confidence that they carried, nobody noticed them. On the road, they could see different horse-wagons. None of them witnessed any cars. Dr. Hamilton conveyed Clark about the way Vroxtal operated. He told him that this part of the north was strange. Every other planet advanced with technological civilization had made everything monotonous. People of Oasis, especially the people of north, they wanted something different, they wanted wagons. Among the hurried currents of wagons, when one stopped, its door came at the exact position where Clark had stood. The white net of the wagon depicted its structure like of a cabin. A young woman greeted him. She had told Clark that she never had seen a man like him. The porcelain layer of her skin, the beautiful women could see that Clark had his eyes on it. But all he was doing was seeing that her legs were tugged under a frock. Her lustrous hair was tied and her skin had become red watching how Clark directly gazed at her eyes. His testosterone filled figure, she felt drawn to it, so much that she asked him if he wanted a lift. Then having her eyes on Dr. Hamilton, she asked: "Is he your friend?"

"Yes," replied Clark. "But it's your wish if you wanna carry him in your wagon."

"Well, that's a nice way to treat someone," said Dr. Hamilton, sarcastically.

There was more than one woman in the wagon. The girl standing at the threshold, she gave a whistle to her friends in the back. They all flickered the curtains on the two windows to have a look at Dr. Hamilton. When they glanced at him, they all nodded their head. He was welcomed to the wagon. He felt a different kind of surrender to them, an intense surrender. He didn't want to call it lust, whereas, all the girls, they were experiencing the same feelings in the presence of Clark, their attention diverted at him. Dr. Hamilton felt a despicable hypocrisy on their part. He knew Clark couldn't do anything about it. They headed to the city of Yanturi.

UNEXPECTED CAN ANYTIME LOOM IN

In the different planets, problems like the AI anarchy was spreading, on some planets, different hackers hacked the system, diseases like virtual eclipses: brain lost in a virtual word, was spreading. These non-conceivable variables of human life—this reign of advanced technological civilizations, more than a boon, it has proved hostile. In far away galaxies, the war of the robots had descended in different planets where their destruction was inevitable. For some planets involving in conspiracies, for them, the chaos of their neighboring planets was considered as an amused indignation. And the planets where annihilation took its birth, the people of those planets were trying hard to fight against the rebellious groups to end their torture. Some had succeeded, some were trying, and some were perished, their planets never to be seen again. Clark, he heard the stories of different planets coming out from the babbling mouth of Emilia. She was the one who had given him and Dr. Hamilton a lift. He was hearing her as if it was necessary in order to maintain that gesture of courtesy—a wagon lift. Everybody was asleep. Dr. Hamilton slept like a man as if he understood the necessity of sleep, bearing the expression of drooling; whereas, all the other girls, they were asleep too. Only Clark and Emilia remained fresh.

Emilia had informed Clark that she was from the south, the city of Oppus where every kind of palaces stood erect. Clark was bored of the traditional characteristics that Oasis as a whole planet carried. He didn't like that the teleportation there was limited, was only allowed if somebody wanted to travel to another planet, or unknowingly, was used if they were welcomed by any attacks; in the case of Clark, it was true, even though teleportation was not allowed during such things, Clark thought that people showed their true color when they feared death. Travelling on the wagon, he concluded that the normal citizens were sloth-like: they moved slow, didn't embrace the advancements of a human brain, just the slow regular imitation of the long, gone century was like a cheap trick to him. He was missing the skyscrapers, the flying cars, and his silent aircraft that few hours ago was roaming over the planet of Oasis, and now, was gone. The only thing that he liked about the wagon was that the horse was robotic, his appearance was elegant like of a real horse, but robotic.

The prairies around him, their expanse of the green and over it the blanket of snow, it reminded him about his great, great grandmother. She was also involved in the war of different worlds. Her name was Natasha and she had spent most of her life on a spaceship. The captain of the ship, traveling through different galaxies, adapting the different cultures of the planet, she had gone back to her roots: against every warning from her colleagues, friends, and people working over her stature, she had fallen in love with the earthean. The way she viewed existence, and the way she viewed man—in every planet, most of them having the attributes as if struck by inferiority complex, spending their time running after women to experience pleasure—Natasha didn't like that. She had visited earth to check the secret base in Kansas. Coming there, it was the first time in her life that she had seen the prairies, so did her introduction with Max. He was the commander in chief of the base. He was placed there because the prairie of Kansas was struck with an UFO object. Natasha came there to study the aircraft. Studying the flying disc in the base gave her the meaning of life. It was not because she was studying the saucer, but it was when love at first sight struck her. She didn't use to believe in such theories, but with Max, theories had turned into practicality. His height, like of a cyber-wrestler; his brain, like of a cyber-hacker, and the way his personality shined, like the firmness of an authentic soldier, this stole Natasha's heart. They had made their first love inside the flying saucer itself, and later on, gave birth to Rick, Clark's great grandfather—an earthean.

He was remembering how great, great grandma Natasha had fought the aliens that had come from a far away galaxy to conquer earth. Her primary job was to travel around different galaxies, to persuade other planets to form an allegiance with earth. But she stayed with Max. She was the most efficient girl at doing her job, but love had conveyed her something more—a bond that couldn't be separated. It was not like that she had abandoned her duties; she fought alongside with her love, whereas, her boss—who had told her stay away from the war and, had asked her, as a matter of fact, had ordered her to just stick to her duties, he didn't want to see

Natasha dead. His order was like the half-whining, half-mad cry of grief. But she didn't listen to him. "She fought," spoke Clark. He was telling this story to Emilia. To him, she resembled the face of Natasha. He had told her that.

"I don't believe you," she replied. Her cheeks were red like a plum. She wasn't used to compliments around this part of a town. Clark in her vicinity, she didn't wonder how he ended up in the planet of Oasis. To her, he looked like a man who depicted a sense of glory—a kind of ruler, not a guard. His veins distracted her. He had rolled the guard's clothes up to his elbow. She thought that Clark was the guy who liked to be challenged. She felt lucky to give him lift. Clark didn't feel the same way. The reason he told her that story was because she did look like Natasha, but her stories about different planets and galaxies, it was like a lullaby—it bored him. But Emilia found joy in his story. She kept on insisting that it was a big compliment that had come from Clark's mouth which she didn't deserve. Then he showed her Natasha's projection—a memory that had come out from her watch, holographically. Watching Natasha talking to her, it shocked Emilia. Lines formed around her forehead when Natasha said: "Clark is right. You do look like me, or I do look like you." It was an AI program that was made to keep ancestors virtually. Satellites around different planets recorded people all the time. This allowed their memories to be stored safely; hence, their AI prototype—its programming in accordance to different memories was possible to bring ancestors alive, not in human form, but just as a show of their holographic display. It was temporary, but it made people feel that they were real. Many court cases enveloped around it. But the discussion of reality in the form of law and order made them lost their cases.

Emilia, talking to Natasha, was baffled. Impressed by Clark, she had never seen a masculine, yet at the same time, an intelligent man. Constantly thinking that she was lucky, she didn't know when her horse took a bump. Her awareness lost inside the wagon, she had forgotten to pay a sharp attention to the route. When she glanced ahead, she saw that the bump was the jammed-up road. A big line of wagons unfolded in front of her. She could see that the guards of Vroxtal were searching different wagons, trying to find somebody. As Clark came to know about it, his expressions got changed. He knew that he could defeat them all, but the noise of fight would bring more attention. To him, doing things in stealth felt like a greater strategy; it didn't produce much physical energy, yet it was an awesome mental exercise. He thought that in order to defeat Dark Storm, he needed to learn different things—to adapt, to increase his artilleries. He told himself that he needed to control the urge of his young blood boiling inside him. But now destiny seemed full of chaos, leaving him no choice as the guards teleported constantly, checking different wagons. They were about to reach them. On the other hand, Emilia could somehow read Clark's expressions. She kind of understood what those expressions meant.

As the guards appeared at the wagon next to her, she had changed the interior decorations of the wagon. The sheets that were white, but at night, had the glow of the moon, it was changed into a pattern of solar-system theme. It allowed the color of Clark's clothes as well as of Dr. Hamilton's to change; from the posh orange clothes, they now appeared like the locals. When the interior theme of the wagon got changed, all the girls had woken up. When the guards came to check upon them, Emilia slammed her mouth into Clark's lips. It was her first kiss. She thought that when things seemed safe, the unexpected could loom in at any time. She told herself that in that time she had to set new order in it to again make things to go smooth. She liked protecting Clark. He knew what she was doing. He was tasting her lips. It had a sharp flavor which made him feel peaceful. All the other girls were one by one kissing Dr. Hamilton. He was waking up slowly. Perceiving his reality from his slumberous eyes, he thought he was still in a dream. As far as the two guards were concerned, they were furious. One of them shouted: "Filthy prostitutes!" resulting both of them to leave their wagon as soon as possible.

As they left, the kissing halted. All the other girls didn't ask any questions. They went back to sleep. Dr. Hamilton was awake. His slumberous eyes were gone. His attention back, he was looking at his friend Clark and that wagon-girl Emilia locking their eyes as if locking the moment.

"Did I miss something?" He spoke, distracting the necessity of their moment. Clark didn't reply him back. He smiled, but that smile was forced, a kind of wince. Whereas, Emilia, she now had her eyes on the route. They headed to Yanturi.

THAT THING!

It took two nights and three days to reach the city of Yanturi. The wagon had stood near the bazaar in the early afternoon. The end of the bazaar introduced an empty garden; the only exception was that the garden had the support of guardians: tripod-like machines, seventy-to-eighty foot tall, stood there. A glittering structure as if having the face of flying mantle, but enlarged, wires dangling from it, and eyes emitting a strong blue light. Dr. Hamilton, his sense of reality, he couldn't perceive the abnormality of the structure. He thought that the people of Oasis had adopted the theme of twentieth century clergyman, but this was new. This was hybrid. Those machines, hovering a bit above the ground, were like the thing of independent judgment. They gave him the actual heebie-jeebies. He told himself to feel calm, when he felt uneasiness seeping in his skin; he told himself that the world was reduced to suffering, but he knew that his default thinking pattern was clogged. Those machines brought the fear out of him. He was aware that both him and Clark, they needed to get past them because before the garden, there was a river. It formed and came from the steep inclines of the mountains, but the point where the water cascaded down, that was the place where the castle had situated itself—in the middle of the waterfall. Clark could see the gigantic spires. They were like hydra-heads to him; if one was down, other was there for its support. He thought in order to kill the heads, he needed to target the main head in between: the purple spire, where the power of teleportation had made its accessibility known.

Clark could see the loving eyes of Emilia. But to her, his eyes was the door to her soul. The gentle lips that she had touched, she felt like she had been reborn. At the first night of their trip, when the guards came to search him and Dr. Hamilton, before touching him, she had already sensed that Clark was not from Oasis. She had stopped her horse-wagon because she felt like the persona of his body had carried a deep gratitude. To that, she had felt sacred throughout her whole journey. Now saying farewell to him, it was like a breakup. She looked at the sky. It had that depth of the blue which indicated love. "We will meet," she said, and whipped her robotic-horse. The wagon was again on the path to complete its journey, leaving Clark and Dr. Hamilton on the bazaar.

The bazaar was like the dreadful place for anybody suffering from claustrophobia. Constituents of being the network of bankers, craftsmen, and merchants, it felt like the chaotic mix of different emotions. In that, both, Clark and Dr. Hamilton, had to maintain anonymity in it. Upon entering the broad footpath, they could see the variety of goods and services being exchanged there. From pots containing weird liquid to wine glasses, from used lightening swords to buckets having God's talking statues, everything implied some kind of a value. All the tents that stood across from each other, they were mingled with light wires. Their clusters at some place was like a clog; below it, there were random, small portals that appeared to be coming from different dimensions. It was more like holographic displays that showed different dragons whirling around its limited sky, but the crowd like a river, they distorted those displays at regular intervals.

People turned to have a glance at Clark as both him and Dr. Hamilton passed. They looked at him, murmured to their respective partners, as if bearing sudden resentment. Clark could give no reason for their behavior; even on earth, people stared at him, giving him those instinct of resentment that his presence arose. And the people in bazaar, they shared the same characteristics. Though the instincts didn't have any impact on Clark, but Dr. Hamilton, his core was shaken out of its ruts. His eyes had the motion of as if he was suffering from an adrenaline rush. At one moment, his gaze was at the tripod-like machines, at another, on the passing crowd. He thought their presence together had an existence of its own, then he spotted the eyes of Clark. He wasn't looking either at the machines, or had any attention on the bazaar. He was staring at the castle. To that, he bore an inexplicable expression. Then his eyes met Dr. Hamilton.

"You said that the castle was on the cliff," spoke Clark.

One of the passers-by heard him. His stout body was fitted under a cotton jacket. His face small, but fat, and his jacket tight, it was pushing out the fats out of his hands.

"It's a shape shifting castle. And the things that you are seeing" —he raised his hand to point out the tripod-like machines— "...that thing is monstrous. That thing! It can suck your blood. They are there because it is said that the castle is in danger. The rumor is that some criminals had escaped the jail from Vroxtal. From Vroxtal! — the place where the most highly skilled guards reside!"

When he said that, the crowd immediate gasped at him and stopped. The person talking to Clark, usually his manners embedded a code of fragility, causing him to get scared easily, but around Clark, he felt an impenetrable security. The crowd had gathered. Among them, listening to that guy, some started having trembling lips; some raised their brows to have an arc between their eyes. His words had affected all. The mixed-up emotions of the crowd, it held indignation, pain, and concern, all at once. The unwashed mass of people, it also brought attention from the tripod-like machines, who at first were standing casually. Now their attention diverted at the crowd, they shot the blue lights from their eyes over the tents of bazaar to assert the situation. The minute that happened, the minute it was that panic seeped into the blood streams of the people. They started running. The blue lights, at first, was just the scanner. When it detected something ill against the normal attributes of being a human being: a sense of danger—it started firing actual beams from its mouth. There were three tripod-like structures. Their beams were like thunder, possessing an intense light, which looking at it, burned the eyes of people. And the men that were hit with the beam, the intense light completed exterminated them.

The destruction had started. Clark, his young blood has boiled up. He told Dr. Hamilton to take care of the people. To that, he took out his sword. As the beams made its way to reach the crowd, Dr. Hamilton with his lightening sword tried its best to reflect the beams back. But the beams were so strong and so many that even if he tried to reflect those beams on the machines, he couldn't able to do it. Either the beams were going back toward the sky, or hitting the nearby mountains, cutting them into different fragments. One even hit the river, causing a maelstrom. The chaos was spreading everywhere like a wildfire. People were hitting each other. Some were blind. Some had lost their closed ones. The emergence of catastrophe had the attributes of hell that had degenerated fast. He was doing what the right men would usually do in this type of situation: protecting the people with his lightening sword. He was doing his best. Meanwhile, Clark was running against the crowd toward those tripod-like machines. Passing the bazaar with his lightening speed, his footsteps touched the garden. He was constantly dodging the beams that came out from the machines. They were now starting to encircle him. Unaffected by it and still running, he jumped at one of them. His hands clenching the dangling wires of the machine, he started climbing toward its top. Reaching there, he smacked his fists through his both hands, blinding the machine. It was still spitting beams of death. But now, having a control of its mouth, Clark directed the head of the machine toward its fellows. Destroying them, the machines collapsed to the ground. And the machine that he stood atop of it, he again jumped from its surface, touching the ground, while it collapsed too.

The crowd was looking at him as he came their way. They all

35

were astonished. When the machines exploded behind him, they all started cheering for him. The cheers had made him stop, causing the crowd and Clark to have some proximity. Then Dr. Hamilton barged in from the mass of people. He was walking fast to stand beside Clark. When he stood toe-to-toe against him, he raised his arm. The crowd cheered again—whistling, clapping, and crying for its savior. Just when everybody was having the moment of bliss, a figure of woman burst in beside Clark. She was as tall as him. Her beauty again brought the gasp from the mouth of the people. As she held Clark's left hand, she immediately vanished, teleporting Clark with her. This all happened in a few seconds. Shock dissolving into Dr. Hamilton's body, the crowd experiencing the same expression, he was left all alone.

    The bazaar was again left to safety. It allowed people to continue their business. After Clark left, nobody was cheering for Dr. Hamilton ever though he protected them. They had turned their back against him and had settled to their tents, carrying the load of their lives. Dr. Hamilton wasn't happy. For a moment, he had thought that those people trusted him, but now safety accompanying them, they showed their true color, he concluded. He was missing Clark. He had to find him to escape this weird planet.

THE MAGICIAN

Diana saw the eyelashes of Clark. This was the first time she had seen a man as bold as him. She watched him, while she carried the awkward excitement of a schoolgirl, but she denied the existence of those emotions, yet she knew she was feeling it. She couldn't able to control it. Diana wished if the people of Oasis were raised the way Clark was raised: fearless. They stood alongside people who were utterly responsible and felt virtuous; especially, the different rulers of various regions. It is easy to look virtuous when you are surrounded by cowards, Diana was thinking. She was standing at the top of a giant statue. Its crown was like an icicle spreading on her direction, while its feet stood across two different lands, separated by a lake below it. The statue had the Greek body. His left arm was raised skyward, holding a flame, just above the crown; another hand was on the long cloth that was wrapped around his waist. Its ending was in the form of a loose drape that came out from his left and reached the end of his foot. Clark's body lay on top of the crown. Beside him was Diana. She was waiting when he would wake up.

The brief teleportation that she had done with him at the time when he had killed those tripod-like machines, it had made him faint. She thought that maybe she lived too close to the purple spire, that her power of teleportation was too strong that made Clark—a non-teleportator, to feel its effects. If she had not teleported him, his brother—Alfred cox, was sending another enemy for Clark. He was called The Magician, not because he liked to do magical tricks, but because he liked to disfigure people's faces. He was neglected by the general population. His body too enhanced with technology, and too flexible that it could change its shape to any animal—people called it monsters, he was considered too dangerous to live among the people. His body almost robotic, it was able to do everything, except the power of teleportation. To do teleportation, the people needed to have a human essence in them—that was the requirement of the portal residing in the purple spire—but The Magician had lost all the components that constituted a human value. Despair hitting him hard, not because he had monsters residing in him, but because he couldn't able to do transportation, even if he wanted to do it, he went to a jungle and lived there.

The way to the castle of Yanturi was the jungle. People usually confused it that the way to the castle was after the garden, but usually, the route was from the jungle. It started from the mountains. The noble people of Yanturi passed it with ease, and the people who weren't noble, their fate met the magician. After that, they were never to be found again. One time, the magician split the person in half. This story revolved around every region of Oasis, causing fear to the normal human endeavours. The stories of the magician started spreading everywhere with contemptuous cynicism retouched by people's gossips. This allowed their fear to reach an optimum level, resulting in only the noble people to go inside the castle of Yanturi—

a shape shifting castle with its shape shifting sceneries, except the route of the jungle where the magician resided. Alfred—the ruler of Yanturi, and the brother of Diana, he made sure to fed the magician. He provided him a mini castle of its own. After hearing about the terrible event in Vroxtal, he had deployed those robotic creatures in case if those fugitives—Clark and Dr. Hamilton, had decided to make their way to his castle. He had also warned the magician to get prepared, only if they escaped those tripod-like machines.

Alfred was an obese man whose mannerisms were retouched by a bit of his educational background. He never wanted to be a ruler, but his father insisted him to purse the course of power. Never understanding the depth of it, he took the opposite way: to cause chaos in the name of his knowledge. Alfred possessed the characteristics of an unknown person who held unlimited power in an undefined position. Having the ability to live more than five hundred years of age due to his mechanic heart, he had become quite belligerent in conducting the royal meetings. In his recent meeting, he talked fashion, instead of the welfare of Oasis; he talked what he wanted, instead of what his noble people wanted. When it came to the normal household people, to them, his welfare consisted of the asserted that "they can survive of their own."

Diana, who was watching the degeneration of bad habits in him, could determine his fate, and that fate, if required its natural ending, was long. She didn't like that he had the power of life or death on people. She had concluded that he had no binding principles to lead the planet of Oasis. All his abilities were delegated; whenever any planet posed any threat to Oasis, Alfred knew that Dark Storm would take care of everything. Even the power the magician held was his indirect gift. The magician was born with some humility, but he had no standard of innocence in regards to his work. The factory he used to work in was devoid of any moral ethics. It dwelled on mediocrity that had consequences both harsh and real. He thought that in order to work in any place standards were necessary, but when mediocrity touches any person, it takes that individual to hell, demands that person to pay a price. Though he worked hard in the factory, but the other workers who talked themselves into irrelevance were usually the ones that depreciated the value of the factory. Even the owner was frustrated. Then one day they all found themselves under an invisible fence, their factory about to get obliterated by the beams shot out from one of the spacecrafts of Dark Storm. He had remembered the way the ship looked—a black, gigantic box, having sharp edges, hovering above them, then the beams of lights accumulating underneath it, obliterating them out of existence.

Daniel Haggard was his name. When death approached him and had wiped him out, the particles of his body were not completely gone. It still surrounded the prairie where that factory was situated. Daniel, since his birth, had done many altercations to his system. The result of it had made him lost his human value—but he didn't know it until the factory blew to pieces, taking all the workers with it. The particles of his body, when it was not completely erased by the nuclear beams, its microcosmic particles that consisted of both electrons and neutrons had a life of its own. At first, they were, of course, non-negligible. Soon, understanding the compatibility of their environment, the particles of Mr. Haggard's body started to develop. When people, passing beside the road of that prairie, started seeing dotes lurking around its surface—those weird looking balls, most of them chose the alternate path. Fear had knocked them down, but some people were reluctant. They chose the same path of their travel.

The fence, and under it, the extermination had caused the stubble to burned out, making a black circle. The radiation automatically was kept under its captivity—a feature provided by the ship's fence, but that harsh environment gave Daniel's cell a new life to regenerate his body cells fast. When they did over a period of time, like a magnet they joined together. His body that time had become like a big skeleton, but it had a life. It rested under that same ground for few months. Nobody had noticed it. The lingering dotes of his particles were gone; the normal people, who feared those, were back. When his bones began to contain flesh, some parts of his bones became charge with energy—a yellow colour bursting with sparkle that travelled around his whole body like a current spreading. Certain people took notice of it; they thought that it was due to the weather man who was converting everything into snow. After almost a year spending under that black circle made by Dark Storm's ship, his body lying there, he finally stood up to his feet. Previously, the symmetry of his face had a proper alignment, but it was quite swollen—an allergy provided by too much mechanic changes in his body; also, resulting his head to have metallic hairs. He looked like a patient whose ability to survival was depended on the enhancements he made, since his birth. But now, as if the nuclear beam shot by the ship of Dark Storm had mutated his body cells, he woke up with his same metallic hairs, but this time, the length of his hair suited his flexible structure. It didn't agitate him. His sunken cheeks—it gave him the depiction of a true sociopath. His killer eyes—it allowed him to obediently fixate his prey. Both hands and legs robotic—now robust, it gave him an ability to run so fast as if he was no longer bounded by a network of social duties. Though he was back, but his rational mind was lost. His only lust was the blood and to crush the bones of any individual who stood across his path.

The first time he took a life was of the fearful hoarders who had forgotten the ball like particles of his body. He took slow steps approaching them. The sky was grey and the black circle caused by the beam had the constant shower of snow. Previously, the radioactive had affected the circle, prohibiting the environment outside of it to cause minor changes to the black circle. But as the new Daniel Haggard approached his first prey, the black circle had started to fade. He was filled with the wish to destroy and devour. The environment around him was surrounded by bits and pieces of ashes; it was matching with the dark colour of the sky. His eyes fixating on the human—a golden light emerging under his pupils, making a line under his eyes, golden sparkles continuing his sunken cheeks, then going all the way to his body, covering his chest, making his abdominal shine—this power, it was making his humanly, but robotic body to change its shape completely. He was converting into a lethal hound. The lower part of his back was growing a tail that was sharp to cut any wings of spaceship. The scales on his back were like icicles about to pierce anything. On top of that, he spit a vicious blade that was attached to his tongue. The blade was poisonous. To touch him was a death. To call that hound just a monster was a shame. Daniel Haggard was bigger than that. The way his four legs touched over the prairie, while melting the showering snow, he charged his victims with his tongued blade. They weren't aware he was coming. His tongue got divided into four, tearing the sheets of the wagons, lifting them up into the mid-air. They were screaming. They were dying slow because the poisonous blade had gone through their chest. They all could see the robotic horses leaving them in a panic-stricken mode. They all thought they were facing the real, deep underworld. This was the last thing that they had remembered. Daniel Taggard in the form of a hound bashed their bodies consistently till they all tore to shreds.

This event spread like a wind when the passers-by saw the tattered parts of their bodies. Even Alfred hearing about him at first was shocked. The only thing that previously shocked him was the army of Dark Storm and Dark Storm himself. But making him an ally, he felt invincible. Hearing about his people getting brutally murdered, this was what was not in his radar. He didn't care about the people, but they dying, it was like slashing a dagger to his power. The havoc of the event even made him dream about Daniel Haggard. The tales of the people gave him the term the magician because of the flexibility of his body to change into any creatures he liked. Phrases like 'the Satan is coming to charge us, or the devil like cruelty' had started becoming normal. People dread nightmares, but if they saw the magician in the nursing fantasy of their bone chilling dream, they pissed their pants. Even though the cells that dwelled inside his body had become powerful; it even had its moments of low. One time killing too much—at that time a monster of fifty foot—he suddenly shrieked into his normal body. That body though—still powerful, still invincible, still knocked down by none, but with it—he felt some kind of principles returning to him. For a month, he halted his hunting. His mind, it was again beginning to work. The perception of his reality, he wanted to find a motive to it. He, for some time, became a teacher in the city of Yorn.

It was the city where Alfred had received his degree. Yorn consisted of different palaces; those palaces constituted of universities; each subject was based on philosophy; those subjects were the different universities. It basically taught the noble people that there was no mind. Professors posed questions like: Why we will be the number one planet? The answer they gave was that power and diplomacy was necessary. Was it practical to use the mind? They had asked and answered: advance technological bodies have the capability to do its function of its own; it didn't require mechanism of any mind. Then they asked the question: Was force necessary? They had answered: Yes, it was, elaborating that force made people harmless and obedient. Then they posed the most philosophical question: was morality the root cause of everything?

—yes! They had answered. These frameworks of the institute defined what Alfred was lacking. He was a slim man that time. He had so many questions about what his teachers were teaching, but their ways of envisioning and shaping the students had left Alfred to get entangled in their thread. He even created hypothetical realms in his mind where real problems of Oasis were addressed, but mind had no use, his teachers had told, only machines that were installed in their bodies were capable of taking care of the human inadequacies.

The institutes stood across from each other. The head of the institute had its own fortress. It was in the middle, situated on the top of the mountain, like the throne of a king. Its left and right laid different palaces, like the perfect synchronization of monarch. When the magician came to meet the head of the institute as a normal man—though most of his parts robotic, but hidden by different designs of clothes; also, the implementation of wintery weather by Dr. Hamilton, now in all the regions of Oasis—he came with convictions: the magician thought that what he had become was unnatural and temporary. He felt that ugliness of his chaos was just mere accidents. He wanted to correct it by discharging his past, saluting his present moment, and confirming his future by the primordial calculator deep residing in him that would keep the balance between that sinful past of his, and that imparting knowledge of the present that the magician was thinking, while he was going to the fortress to meet the head.

The fortress had huge brick walls. The colour of it was white; it was made up of marbles. Only while flourished around the fortress. When he reached his office, two statues of gargoyles stood across the door. Upon entering it, he saw the head sitting on his chair; the light of the sun, which was mild, hitting from the window, reaching the head's desk. It made his bald head to have an exclusive shine, his gut which was about the size of any lady's labour day, the head felt comfortable in it. He had brown moustaches that covered the upper part of his lips; his ears were long. His hands didn't contain flesh; they were purely metallic; it matched with the color of the marble. The undersized torso had the support of oversized legs. His name was Luther Cox. He was the father of Alfred Cox. The peculiar glance of his eyes watched the magician as if he was contaminated by a revulsion. Meanwhile, the magician's sunken cheeks, his metallic hairs—which was partially tucked back, giving him an appearance of having a natural hair on his head—and everything covered by a strange dress code, Luther just observed him. His pupils closed, he talked his principles.

"Why are you here?" he asked. "I see you don't have any resume."

"I'm here to teach the meaning of spirit to reclaim mine," the magician had answered with his raspy voice. Luther Coz could feel the calm in his voice, but he knew—or he felt, that there was something buried deep inside him whose manifestation was the outer appearance of his clothes. He was flung with emotions, not the type of emotions that he gets when he sees his other teachers. Those emotions, which contained no essence of the words, looking at the magician, he wanted to question his conscience, so he asked: "Can you define what is a spirit?"

"It is a light residing in all of us. I have lost mine. Somehow, its back—just a small spark of it. I wanna reclaim its depth. Is this the right institution?"

"My boy! Real spirit is intolerable to the pure soul. It is tainted here. Don't waste your time," spoke Luther.

The magician thought that to conceive a vision, it needed practice. Somehow, his too much killings had created a plateau to bring his logic back to some state, causing him to rationalize about the way Luther viewed existence. He thought he lacked vision because it was expensive, concluding that wisdom couldn't be bought by enhancements. The magician was paying attention to him. Luther's voice was like as if an inch of his tongue was cut; to that, his syllables were disturbed, but people understood him. Hearing Luther as if hearing him in a way to later on forget his words into an unnoticed background, like fading, he suddenly questioned the perception around his viewpoints on life: "You don't understand. I want to surpass my temptations. Don't you wanna considered spirit an additional subject of philosophy?"

"You can say the same thing about mysticism."

"Well, I can teach that too," replied the magician. To that, Luther went silent. He thought that the magician came with an incorrigible wit; he had not thought about returning back, empty hands. He was aiming what his consciousness was telling him at the moment: what he thought about life corresponded to what life really was. The magician just required a chance at that. Feeling that, Luther wanted to be a helper, to play the role of an initiatory to give the magician a chance.

"You know," he said, "the way Oasis works, it requires that ruthlessness. Will you be able to withhold that self-ignorance in that ruthlessness?" asked Luther.

"I don't get you," spoke the magician.

"You have to follow my instructions whenever I will come to give it them to you…even if I'm wrong."

The magician thought for a minute, then uttered: "Yes, of course."

"You get the job then…to teach spirit as a subject. Every subject have different palaces. I will construct one for you. It will be done in a matter of few hours."

"Thank you," spoke the magician and left.

He was carefully observing everything, communicating with the students just to scrape the surface of his beliefs. With focus, talking with the noble people, he thought that their actions defined what their inner belief was. To that, he felt indifferent; especially, to their pride. He thought that something had gone wrong. The value of their product: their enhanced bodies, they were very unskilled at humanly interactions, just like him. But he was trying; they weren't. He was finding something to begin with, but the students, they hadn't at all aligned themselves with the truth. They just depended on the betterment of their enhancement, not their soul. At least, he was trying to find what his sudden logic was doing to him. It told him to focus on the day, not tomorrow, to practice to live in the present moment, to see and comprehend what was present to him in front him to understand the world.

The new palace where spirit as a subject of philosophy had to be teach was created. Upon teaching the students—the noble people, he found out that for them the laws of Oasis were quite stretchable, while for the people who couldn't afford the price to study in these palaces, to them, the laws were rigid. Even the students who had their parents serving the regime of Alfred Cox—if they mistakenly teleported themselves—fictional tale were developed, telling the police that their teleportation was a necessity, but in reality, it was just for fun; to that, they were usually excused. While, the normal household people, who had the power of teleportation, but if used, were thrown to prison for eternity, their life was over. The magician saw that the students followed the forms of expression exercised as a law that had been discovered long ago by Alfred's ancestor. The social corruption was at top most that caused the cultural reconstruction to assume a tyrannical change. This caused the huge gap between the nobles and the normal people. While they worked in different factories, the noble students attended their palaces in the name of practicing philosophy. But something drastic had happened since the magician took over new palace where he taught the subject spirit.

"Every human has the ability to create his form, meaning, and goal." —this was the first sentence uttered by his mouth. Though the students attending him were few because of his peculiar persona, but they heard him clear and loud. His way of articulation had caused a sudden change in their mind. The few students, they had never seen a teacher like him. His words stuck in their mind, they conveyed the same to their fellow students. The next time, the crowd of students had doubled. "What is expression? It is the motor of your soul that gives your body a chance to improve." —this second phrase—a starting line of the second lecture, it had caused the students to understand that they had to travel their own road by taking their own steps. The only difference was that the road was same, but their steps taking that same road, it would allow their journey to be different. Those students—watching for the first time their brain to absorb something, they spread their word to mouth to everyone they would meet. "What are rules? —there are no rules for the soul, or else, we would all be the same!" —this was the first phrase he started out in his third lecture. Listening to the magician, the attending students had tripled. This had caused chaos in the mind of other teachers, causing resentment and jealously. It puzzled them. In front of him, they always showed their friendliness, but inside, they dwelled the monster mindset of a criminal. They were curious. They were hit by the way he created an attractive atmosphere where civility among the students was practiced. Talking with him, their hearts had persuaded, but their mind was telling them to not fall for his eloquent mannerisms.

"A mind is a tool for the soul. They are not separated. One has to understand that." —this was the first phrase of the starting of his fourth lecture. The time, his classroom was full. All the students were familiarized with him. His peculiar persona: his full body covered with fancy clothes till neck, it was fading under their eyes, only his words made long lasting impact. Listening to him, they started to have their own opinion, so does their way of life. Their life monotonous with enhancements, they wanted something different. While forming new opinions of their own, they had also developed the sense that they couldn't question or criticize the power ruling over them: the regime of Alfred Cox. They all had started to seek something, and that something was the magician words. It was like literal magic to them. Whenever the students left his classroom, they couldn't wait for the next lecture. His means of teaching were spreading around the different regions too. The magician—who was considered as a monster, who was considered anonymous, his tales of brutality had started to vanish too. Daniel Haggard—the new teacher, was the new name that people had on their lips.

"What a human think of itself, so does becomes his fate; same thing happens with his soul—his spirit." —this was the first phrase of the starting of his fifth lecture. By that time, his classroom had extended. The benches of students were enveloped into a long depth, but it nothing to his voice. It was clear, bold, and sharp. His new logic, it took his body. Students, who were first scared of his weird clothing style, they started liking the way the magician got dressed, like an actual magician. He wore an orange suit, his hands covered with black gloves, complimenting his black shoes, along with the cloth wrapped around his neck—all these things gave him an identity, like a brand forming. When he was a monster, he went from a desperate city, to desperate regions to console his bloodlust crimes, but now, that unconsciousness disappearing, his new identity was giving him a recognition. Though still a rigid man, forbidden by temptations, he had started to like his new found fame. "It is never too late to give up our preconceived notions." —this was his first phrase of the starting of the sixth lecture. All the students who used to attend different palaces to study different subjects, they now all attended his lectures. It seemed like they had left their ancient ways of teaching and had now demanded their brain to function in order to align with their soul by attending the magician's lecture. It was like what their old teachers had made them learn, a smoke of cloud, promising them that smoke of cloud would sprinkle a fertilizing shower of rain on their field, all the students had considered that it was a falsehood idea and had discarded it.

"Old ways are for the old people; new discoveries are for the new people." —this was the first phrase of the starting of his seventh lecture, the end of the week. By this time, all the students of different palaces, even all the teachers, including the head: Luther Cox, were present in his lecture. They heard him. They listened to him, carefully. They were attracted to his mannerisms, but intentionally denied the existence of such feelings. They didn't like that he was telling life as an experiment. They were terrified that he was telling the students that million things could go wrong at any second in the planet of Oasis—this was how he conveyed the definition of life. Indirectly, he was conveying them how to organize a brain, how it was so important—or else, it gets drawn into short-term gratifications: instead of seeking out the meaning to calm anxiety, the mind seeks out comfort, instead of seeking out the meaning to defend suffering, the mind ponders over criminality; he was lecturing that. But for all the teacher, to them, his studies of sprit were conveying them that he was telling the students how to be mortal. To old teacher, all the students were immortal, so did their ways of teaching: pride enhanced subjects disguised as different subjects of philosophy. They knew that their students were ought to live more than thousands of years, and perhaps, would conqueror planets, and to old teachers, it was immortality, not pity mortality.

The magician thought that to tell them the truth was important, not in the way to convey the language of direct mysticism, but with plain, simple truth. Patiently. Gently. The way he had gripped the students, the old teachers never had performed that kind of magic in over a decade. Their eyes at him was full of revulsion, like an act of dominance. In the outer manifestation of their gestures, they had acknowledged him by giving him a smile, but under their loathing soul, they had given that same smile an act of unforgiveness. They all hated him so much that they couldn't control his bold voice. To them, each word coming out from his mouth was like an actual dagger, enhancing the depth of their hatred toward him. Even their part-robotic bodies, the wires dwelling inside it were over charged.

They all couldn't control it; as the lecture wasn't ending, for them, was too long—a voice of Luther Cox halted the magician's words. All the students looked at the head.

"What kind of twisted sense are you teaching?" he asked.

"Spirit," he answered. The class laughed to that, except the teachers. Watching all the teachers furious, the smile of all the students vanished.

"Now, from today onwards, the palace of spirit will be dissolved"—the students were anger, they were making noises to Luther's words—"and Mr. Haggard will be fired. Please maintain the silence." No one was maintaining the silence. Then Luther Cox fired a mild beam from his palm, damaging the podium through which the magician was teaching. This was the first time that the magician had got the touch of anger in over a month. But he told himself to be relax. He looked at the head with a smile, while showing a sense of a patient person. But the head, he continued: "Now you all are silent. What I was saying? …yes! Mr. Haggard is fired. His palace will be dissolved as soon as you all will leave and—

"And he will not get fired. He will continue his teaching." —a voice came from the crowd of students. There was one other person too who was present other than the staff of teachers. It was Diana Cox, sister of Alfred Cox. She had felt peace between among other teachers, among their eruption of revulsion. She had looked at the magician, directly at his eyes; those eyes had conveyed him: Don't worry. For a moment, the lock of their eyes had faded the background of students and the older teachers. Catching her eyes, the magician had understood that Diana was something different. She was definitely was a noble person, but she carried the characteristics of a practical woman who grace life as a call to go beyond it, as in higher than the Oasis adultery and not to be regarded as a tainted symbol of the planet. The eyes conveyed him that, and her smile, it told him of Diana's impurity.

"But Diana, he is breaking every rule of the philosophy."

"That's life, dad."

"But as a head, I can't let that happen!"

"I think we should let the students to adapt to the nature of Oasis, so that they can develop their strength by understand their spirit," when she uttered her last words, she glanced back at the magician. He retuned her the smile.

"Alright!" Luther said. All the teachers got up from their desk, surprised. "Alright! Let him teach what he preaches," he looked at the magician, "spirit! But I will ask him to tell all the students to attend their other teachers too! They are breaking the law of different palaces!"

"Sure," answered the magician. "I will convey them now. Students, do attend their lectures. If you don't it, attend it. I will promise you that I will purify everything that you will dislike."

"Enough!" exclaimed Luther. "Don't be over smart. Simplify yourself. Don't be like your clothes, overcoating even the words.

You just are lucky. Remember that you will not be always."

All the teachers, including Luther Cox were leaving. Diana stayed with the students, while the magician finished the lecture. The eyelashes of Diana had the power to lure everybody; the flickering gaze of students were constant at her. Her face—as if a product of milk, her blue eyes—as if a universe residing in her, her body—as if a perfect combination of strength and power induced with cuteness, it was like nature was taking well care of her. She seemed like a person who was carefree to know what she knew, and what she did not know, she did not know. Diana's face had the illumination of that. For the first time, it was hard for the magician to take her eyes of her. He was aware that he was mostly a machine, but, as if preaching good habits for the first time to burn his sins, he felt like people were attracting to him. If he can happen to him, it can happen to anybody, he told himself. But didn't expect girl like Diana sitting at his lecture, looking at him. He told himself that it was to okay to let his heart beat, not to feel ungrateful by it; he told himself that he shouldn't be astonished, when he felt some kind of drive inside him. A drive—he thought—a desire, he filtered his thoughts, it was like a new engine that was residing inside his body, showing a different life.

Completing his lecture, he went outside of the palace. The different routes collecting different palaces, he was observing them. The magician was conscious and he didn't carry any reactions with him. He was present and so was Diana when she came and stood beside him. At first, he didn't realize it. He felt too much into the nature, even if it was artificial: covered by a blanket of snow. As soon as his gaze whirled at her, their glance touched again. They again locked; her glance was a spark of serenity; his was of happiness. Now those eyes meeting were like exchanging of the energies. It was just like a positive emotion, when you possess it, the world reflects those feelings back at you—the pair of the magician and Diana was like that. She thought that the magician was a man of self-respect; he would not bend to any people, even if he wanted to.

Diana attended his every lecture. But the other teachers were crumbling. They hated him, so did Luther Cox. He went to his son after the end of his week's lecture. But all Alfred was doing was studying the havoc of creatures who killed his people in different regions. The people working for him wasn't able to find those monsters residing in one person: the magician, but he made an effort to dive himself into studying the patterns of those creatures. He found out that the man had the ability to change his body to anything, anything vicious. This shapeshifting quality, this was what his castle had, and the sceneries surrounding it. He got that ability because of Dark Storm—as a gift to protect his castle as some kind of a labyrinth for the intruders to get lost. But this familiarity, he attached that with the magician shapeshifting quality to any creature. In the palace he was known as Mr. James Haggard, and in different regions—a magician, now a perishing name. Alfred was looking for him; he had two ideas in his mind that he wanted to execute; first was to destroy him, second was—a non-negligible possibility, to make him an ally.

When his father came at him to tell him his new intersection of life with a strange human, Alfred wasn't interested. He just wanted to find the magician. He was sending his spies as the motors of his world had been stopped. He also knew that he couldn't call Dark Storm just like that. He was only available when threat was imminent on the planet of Oasis; also, telling him about the magician was like telling him a plan of how to damage his reputation. Even though the shapeshifting qualities were some kind of commonalities to him, he avoided asking Dark Storm any matter regarding of the tragedy that had happened in Oasis, in cold blood. Alfred's mind focused at one thing, he avoided all the other things, including his father. Finding no success, he then listened to him, not when he mentioned about the magician, but when his father told him about the way Diana was falling for him. To that, Alfred was surprised. She was the kind of girl to him that didn't perceive the attributes of how Oasis worked. Her face usually had the expression of constant-ignorance whenever it came to ruling the planet of Oasis. Diana wanted things different, and Alfred didn't like that. He had chosen his best soldiers, told secretly to make them fall in love her, indirectly changing her ideology if she fell for anyone of them. But none had worked. To accept that she was falling for a weird looking man who wore fancy clothes, like a magician, usually more than the noble people to hide his maybe enhanced robotic body parts, he thought that there was a catch there; Alfred thought he should be cautious; he should search. Thanking his father, Alfred went to attend his lecture.

Whenever he listened to long speeches, the obscenity of his skill sets always allowed him to eat something, while he listened. This thing wasn't noble, but to him, it had become noble because he was taking care of everything in the planet of Oasis. The self-revelation of his ugliness, he made no efforts to conceal what he was doing in the classroom. He never blamed his body; he never blamed the installed mechanisms inside him, giving his tongue sensors an extra ability to something as best in the universes, producing that dopamine effect that was more pleasurable than anything else in different worlds. That body enhancement, he could have done the same about sensual pleasures, but he denied those sinful things to happen with him because he didn't want to get entangled with any women. For his mind, it was like jeopardizing his kingdom in the name of democracy. But inside the classroom, showing disrespect to the magician, while he listened and ate a sandwich, it didn't infuriate him, that effect was experienced by Diana. Her face was red. She thought that power had the ability to turn any weasel into a fake, bold figure. She didn't like that he was shielded from pain, or fear, hindering his abilities to learn more. When the magician completed his lecture, Alfred got up and told him that when next time he would give lecture, he had to wear a normal t-shirt.

"Alfred, what are you doing?" exclaimed Diana.

"I'm doing what my mind is telling me. Palaces follow a proper code of clothes. Just look at what he is wearing," replied Alfred.

"Just look at what he is saying."

"We, the people of Oasis, follow customs. Those customs define us; without them, what we are?"

"Even including the way you ate a sandwich, disrespecting him?" spoke Diana.

"You know that I'm facing this problem since birth."

"You mean pleasure."

"Don't overstate things, sister," he spoke, then looked at all the students, also, at the magician, "He will only teach when he will follow the customs of our planet. Who are you? Where did you come from? —these questions, I don't expect answers from you. As a matter of fact, I don't need answers. I just need you to wear a plain t-shirt, that's it, and you will have your job," said Alfred and left the classroom.

After the lecture, for the first time, Diana had seen him upset outside the palace. She wanted to ask him questions, but she let him dwell on the elements of what he was conceiving as being upset. She wanted him to feel it for some unknown reason. Then inside her mind a thought came behind that unknown reason; she wanted to him to learn something from feeling upset. She knew that it was usually upset things that makes someone stand tall. Diana was looking at him like that. When his eyes glanced at her smiley face, it made him forget the reason why he was upset. They watched the environment around them: the palaces. Then Diana asked him a question: "Will you come with me?"

"Where?" said the magician.

"Library," she replied. To that, he gave a chuckle. Then she spoke, "It is in the jungle. Are you coming with me?"

She was going and he was following her. The jungle was way behind the fortress of Luther Cox; it was way behind the mountains. She teleported her with him; she knew it was illegal, but for him, she bent the laws. The library was surrounded by tall trees; it was in the form of a hut. But when they went inside it, the magician saw so many books inside it that he couldn't fathom how the size of the hut was supporting all these books. Then Diana conveyed him that the hut was underground; she told him that this library had all the answers. The magician was looking around the different shelves to read different titles of the book. From the ground floor, he went to the deepest section of the hut. Reaching the last shelf—as if hiding, but in actuality too deep into finding the answers to kill his monsters, he finally read the title: The Code Of Shapeshifting. When he opened the book, the view of the galaxies explored around him; the blanket of universes over his head was pointing out all the starts where shapeshifting mechanisms occurred. He then touched the planet of Oasis; there he learned that the castle of Alfred had the shapeshifting qualities, so did his surroundings. Finding out the history gave him the history of Dark Storm: how he provided him his castle different shapeshifting powers. Only that, nothing much about Dark Storm. The magician could see the event through the book where Dark Storm was sending his army of nuclear engineers who were creating programs in order to create the shapeshifting lands; the tectonic plates inside, its reaction once made the planet of too hot. It allowed the people to wear less clothes, exposing their enhanced bodies, but kidnapping Dr. Hamilton—the weather man, everything got changed. Watching the event above his eyes, he saw that the shifting sceneries were only halted when the purple spire—where the source power of teleportation resided, ignited. To him, that purple spire was some kind of cure to him. He felt that accessing the power of the spire would cure his dwelling monsters.

Diana, when she found out that the magician was lost in his findings, she thought that she was finding something to cover some kind of hidden sanity. Then she saw the shapeshifting exploration of his. To that, she came near him, quite close. Instead of asking him what he was really trying to do, their lips locked each other; their eyes, which had the same moment of eroticism before, now it got shut. He took her above the board of shelves while they kissed. Her back slumped against there and her legs spreading just below his torso, Diana had closed her eyes. Meanwhile, the magician's eyes, its pupils, they had started to glow. Golden lines were forming a straight line between his sunken cheeks. They were going to his abdominal, making it glow with the golden colour too. His mouth still slammed into her, he was unbuttoning her white tulip with his right hand. Her arms enveloped around his neck, she started doing the same thing too. When he caressed her breasts, she gave a loud moan, but in that moment, she bit her lips too in order to numb the noises of pleasure. Her normal hands, somehow, it reached to his fancy trousers. She was successful in unbuttoning it and The Magician was successful in pushing his torso in between her skirt. To that, Diana closed her eyes tight. Her hands were feeling the heat of his neck, simultaneously, were also roaming around his body in a plea to counter her moans. The shimmer of the belt wrapped around his fancy jean, now reaching his thighs, it kept distracting Diana. But whenever her attention was diverted for a split-second, The Magician's mouth went deep into hers.

KNOWING THE TRUTH

Alfred going back to his castle after leaving the lecture of The Magician, he was thinking. He could have teleported, but he followed the rules other people followed about teleportation. He thought that the essence of The Magician's words—in his mind, Daniel Haggard—was having the reflection on his body, which made him conclude the logical faculties of students. Their parents, who mostly worked for Alfred, had told him that their children were behaving properly. They had lost their pride. They had lost their temperaments, and it made all the parents somehow happy. Observing The Magician when he was giving the lecture, his clothes, it made Alfred wonder about the gone shapeshifting monsters—their disappearance, and the sudden appearance of the magical Daniel Haggard. It made him question that the timings were quite off. Those two personalities are totally different, he said to himself, while he made his way. He really wanted the man whose body resided different monsters. He was thinking about asking Dark Storm. His presence was constantly knocking the door of his mind. The monsters of The Magician, its first traits made him to crawl into his past: Alfred had gone to the black circle, where a factory was destroyed by the ship of Dark Storm. The ship had killed all the people working inside it, along with the factory. He had helped the subordinate ship of Dark Storm by erasing the documents of all the people there who had died. He didn't know their names. He wished if he knew them.

Reaching his castle, he felt for the first time that something was amiss in it: whenever he entered it, he felt perfect. But now, he felt incomplete. He was not able to understand the puzzle he was in. This was also his first time that he had used his brain to find someone. He again concluded that perhaps the words of Daniel Haggard were still working on him. On the other hand, he couldn't resist to call Dark Storm. He wanted his external thing: the betterment of Oasis, to be in synchronization with his mind. That external thing was like an external heat—access fuel, which was more than his own internal heat, cooking the chemistry of his mind to go nowhere. Alfred couldn't resist that he would never find the man behind those monsters. To that, his emotions were erupting. He couldn't control his resistance, so he made a call to Dark Storm. His allegiance to many of the planets, it was like a bond. He had the ability to feel their urgency, so he felt what Alfred was looking for. Busy conquering a planet, he sent out his subordinates: that same ship who created the fence around that factory, destroying everyone.

The subordinates consisted of four people. The captain's name was Alex Stutheart. He gave Alfred all the documents. Among the list of the factory members that he had installed under a chip of his forehands—one of the many chips constituting some kind of a memorial in his arms, it was providing Alfred the holographic display of their faces. The faces were automatically swiping under a gap of five seconds. When he saw the face of Daniel Haggard, he told Alex to freeze the face. The current Daniel had a very different frame of face, and the previous one had the attributes of a synthetic farmer: cheeks swollen by allergies, weak arms, eye brows thinned out, and the overall outlook like of a labourer. But Alfred Cox could identify him, even if the face didn't match that much, but his name did. And that was enough. Though he wasn't surprised that his doubts—at first so inaccurate comparing these two different personalities, had proved right. But astonishment came in when he realized that his sister had fallen for him.

He didn't inform Alex about his sister. He told him about the shapeshifting monsters residing in The Magician, whose name now he knew was Daniel Haggard. Then the captain of the ship: Alex Stutheart answered him that the beams of his ship had produced reactions inside the bodies of different humans living in different planets. He narrated a story informing about the effects of the nuclear fusion beams that had been installed in his spaceship, that it had made monsters before. The previous planet that he had conquered around the region of Proxima Centuri, their people too were obsessed with enhancements in their body; some people were too much it that they wanted to establish an AI monarchy that would run their planet virtually, would also be able to connect different planets of different galaxies with ease. When he destroyed that planet with his ship, the people who did enhancements since birth, just like the magician, after the destruction of their planet, they were turned into monsters. But they weren't shapeshifting, he told Alfred, meeting his eyes. "They spit beams. They jumped high. That planet had become the planet of the monsters. Very few though, but vicious monsters, who loved their territory, were quite tribal and hostile. We didn't need to worry about them. They fought themselves to death," Alex spoke.

"But what we can do about him?" spoke Alfred, telling him about the magician.

"We can do many things," answered Alex. The display of Danial Haggard: The Magician, over his arms, he touched his face. The moment he touched it, the moment it was that his whole body got displayed, the body before the reaction of nuclear fusion. Studying the anatomy of the body, he quickly found out that The Magician's body structure was changed when he was born by his mother. The chance of his survival was near negligible, so she gave him an iron-bone injection, capable of creating new, strong bones, and a new channel of blood stream. As he grew up, that channel produced a different kind of blood whose elements were changed, reacting with the normal blood that his heart still produced. It gave him the swollen cheeks and all the abnormality that his body faced, but after the nuclear fusion beams hit him, it regenerated the cells of his body fast, the cells that first made his bone structure to survive. The beams wiping out his body resulted in eliminating the normal blood that his heart pumped and only produced the kind of blood that his body needed after his body cells showed a chance of survival by floating in the form of dotes over the prairie.

"So what can we do about it?" asked Alfred.

"The cells that his body have, they are like evil, real evil. Those want something. I think he had killed many people. The appetite of those cells is full. We need to bring back the appetite," said Alex.

"How?"

"We just need to attach a bacteria to his body that will evoke the cells to hunt again," spoke Alex.

"Well, how do you proposed to do that?" asked Alfred, wincing.

"We have a machine. Actually, it's a monster too. Find The Magician and we shall send the our monster."

Alfred walked to his throne. Behind it was the portal of teleportation. Through it, he could see the expanse of the forest, leading up to the library where The Magician was making out with Diana. As soon as he saw his sister, his flat palm came over his face. That reaction was involuntary. The fate of their lives was predestined in his eyes. He wanted one dead, and he wanted one chained. Witnessing the scene, purple light flared under his eyes. The same colour the portal of teleportation emitted. The scene had hit him so hard that his body hovered over the ground.

"Unleash the monster! And Kill The Magician!"

CRUEL FATE

Diana and The Magician, as they made love, they could hear something outside of the library. Some kind of a loud, thumping noise that was approaching them. Realizing that there were hardly any parts that was human in The Magician, Diana finally asked him: "Who are you?" To that, he answered: "I'm that monster who was killing everybody in Oasis." Diana wasn't shocked. She knew something about him was special; she just didn't know that speciality came in the form of preaching criminality. "But I'm no more of that," he spoke, assuring her of his current method of being a teacher as a permanent profession. But the outside noises worried him, not in a way that those noises would harm him, but in a way that those noises wouldn't able to do any harm to Diana. Looking at him, she understood that form of unconfessed form of worry. But she listened to him, even though she had the power to defend herself.

He went outside, telling Diana to remain where he was reading the book: The Code Of Shapeshifting. When he came outside the library, he saw no one. The moment he turned around, he got hit with a mechanic tentacle pulsating with current. His body dragging a few metres away, he saw a tri-pod like machine, but here, too high, reaching more than one hundred fifty feet. The tress around that machine were like pencils. Here the tentacles too were too many.

The face of the machine constituted like of a giant ant. The compound eyes were blinking red, while the sharp mandibles were ready to tear The Magician in half. As it charged him with another tentacle, The Magician dodged it perfectly. His body wasn't changing to any monsters, even if he wanted to. The machine's tentacles coming at him were non-stop. He constantly escaped the brutality of their grip. Then somehow, he was able to mount a wheel around his left hand. The spikes around it, they started to whirl fast like some kind of a grinding machine. He was able to cut the tentacles, causing a fragile spark, as they came at him. He was running fast toward the machine. Still, the tentacles charged him. Still, he cut them. As he took a jump like a leap of faith over the machine, the sharp mandibles had spread themselves to snap his body in half, but before that, in under a second, instead of lighting his body with a beam, the machines spat some kind of a chemical on his face. As far as the mandibles were concerned, they couldn't able to catch The Magician. With a sharp wheel running over his left hand, he was able to cut the machine in half. The blasting effect of it had his body to get thrown just beside the library, from where he took his run to kill that gigantic machine.

He was lying flat on the ground. His hands were over his face. His body was constantly convulsing. The vicious pain inside his body made him shout. The shout was not like a plea for help, but it was kind of some way to endure the pain he was suffering. He couldn't stop the jitters that caused inside his body. The spinning wheel that was attached to him had come off. When Diana out, listening to his voice, she dropped to her knees. Tears were rolling down her cheeks. The right hand of her covered her mouth in order to control the constant sobs. She couldn't endure the tight groans coming out from his mouth.

"Just go!" The Magian shouted. "I'm no more Daniel Hargga—" He started growl, as if he had lost the language of words.

His body was expanding. First were the arms that were getting bigger; the brown hair of colours spreading over it were wires. Then the next was his legs; same thing happened there. As his hands left his face, the whole face of his was corroded. Flesh was coming out of it. His teeth were sharpening; the canines were passing his lower lips. He was becoming the actual definition of The Magician, that phrase which the people had remembered: "the Satan is coming to charge us, or the devil like cruelty." Seeing him almost converted into a monster, in fear, Diana fled, but her legs got caught under his arm. Then she tried to teleport herself. She couldn't able to do it. Instead of the teleportation, she could see the absorption of current pulsating over the arm of The Magician. Diana thought that she was dead when she was a ten feet monster stood above her eyes. As he opened his mouth, saliva dripping down, while a weird smell released from there, a horn had hit the castle of Yanturi. The sound of it had distracted The Magician. Now, he was without his logical faculties. Leaving Diana, he ran tearing the forest.

THE DRAGON'S BELLY

It was two years ago that The Magician had left Diana, but to her, it seemed like yesterday. She knew that after he had left her, he went straight to the castle of Alfred where he tried to access the power of teleportation. Couldn't able to do it, he again went to the forest, lived where the hut: library, of Diana was situated. The Magician made that library his home. Though he killed the people, but he spared the life of those who visited Alfred. This helped him create a tale that The Magician was his friend, given to him by Dark Storm himself. In actuality, nobody knew why he killed regular household people. On the other hand, Alfred also had forgotten about binding Diana in chains and locking her up in a jail. The turnaround of events had made him so happy that he didn't care about his sister. In his mind, he was saying that she could now do anything; it would not affect him. But now, she was looking at Clark. Something about him made her think that she needed to better herself. She could see that there was something pure in him as he was lying over the statue. She was waiting for him to wake up. As his eyelids twitched a bit, as if trying to bring a creative brain back to life, it brought some kind of spark in her. When he finally opened his eyes, like bringing interest and magic to life—the type of magic where he destroyed those tri-pod like machines and made Alfred angry again, to worry—she glanced at Clark with gentle admiration.

Standing on his feet, his eyes fell on her. For a second, her beauty struck him, then he realized where he was standing. On his left side, he could see the shreds of lands around him; on his right, the continuation of the mountain that he had seen when he destroyed those tri-pod like machines in the garden, before the bazaar.

Making his way to one of the pointy hooks of crown, sitting there, he asked Diana: "Who are you?"

"Careful there. The crown can break," she replied.

"If it breaks, it will land me under the ocean. I'm a good swimmer. Will you join me there?"

The casualness of Clark made her a bit nervous. And she was never nervous. She watched him as if adrenaline had been injected inside her. His smile made her heart to beat louder. She had never felt this kind of sensation, even with The Magician. The expression of Diana amused Clark.

"Are you the same person who locked my friend for seven years in jail?"

Diana felt her cheeks hot. Her eyes flickered constantly. She had known Dr. Hamilton before, long before The Magician, but she was also aware that Dr. Hamilton was not capable to defeat Alfred alone, to access the portal that gave him and everybody else the power of teleportation. Diana didn't want to watch a poor soul die, so she had conveyed Dr. Hamilton that she would help him to access the portal, but instead had called him in an attic of one of the castles near the purple spire, telling guards to arrest Dr. Hamilton, putting him in jail for seven years. But finally witnessing a man who was capable to defeat Alfred, and also, The Magician, Diana knew that she had to put an accelerated effort for Clark to realize his purpose.

"What are you thinking?" said Clark.

"I don't want you to injure yourself."

"Why are you caring for me?"

"Because," said Diana, "The Magician was waiting for you. You can't defeat him like that. You need practice."

She unfolded the tale of different shapeshifting monsters residing in him and how his acts provided stability to Alfred. Diana knew that her fling with The Magician was past. Daniel Haggard was dead; the new identity inside him, she didn't know anything about it. She told herself that she had to look ahead in life and she was doing that while she watched Clark's face, expecting some kind of a reply from him. But in his mind, he was thinking that the fight with The Magician was inevitable. He understood why she teleported him after his fight with the tri-pod like machines. Looking at her blue eyes, he could see that she was gathering some kind of a courage, but he could conclude that she was broken inside. Even if she had the power of teleportation, her state stayed the same. He understood her urgency to heal. He was like that before Dark Storm burned his eyes. After coming back to life, he was comprehending how it was very important to cope up with his young blood: the power of his inner ignition itself that wanted to achieve everything fast. With

Diana, thought Clark, he would achieve longevity. He thought that they would both improve together. He could see that same enigma inside of her, a bit tainted, but enough for someone to make an argue inside their mind that Diana was something. And Clark had to find that.

"What kind of practice are you talking about?" he spoke.

"Every region has got something that we can learn from."

"What about this region?" asked Clark.

"You said that you were a good swimmer."

"Are you asking me to jump?"

"Yeah," replied Diana. "Don't you wanna meet those giant fishes who destroy ship with their synthetic tails?"

"What?" exclaimed Clark.

"Now jump. I will follow you."

His eyes were light and intelligent. The corners of his mouth were upturned. Diana could see that Clark had attached some gentle and generous quality to him. She thought he wasn't afraid of anything, that's why those qualities came naturally to him. She could see the classical perfection of his head matching with his smile. But Clark, he didn't glance back at her, he observed the area of Clinis standing on the ring of the statue and dived. The lake had the crystal layer; it was frozen, but he didn't care. His head like of an adamantine diamond, he broke the crystal layer of the lake. The clash didn't hurt him. When he was inside the lake, he was waiting for Diana. The world around him was a bit dark and blueish resembling a gloomy night. He was looking at different creatures. All artificial. The robotic structures of different fishes in front of his eyes, they were like moulded shapes of metal that were converted into different shapes of fishes. The aquatic life was mesmerising. The fishes were friendly. Some had red beeps over their head, indicating their life span. From medium length to about the size of his finger, all fishes were fast. Suddenly, witnessing the color of the water changing: from dark bluesish to a stronger color, and all the fishes disappearing, Clark thought that something was wrong. Also, the colour of the lake didn't change completely. He could see his far left and right corners retaining the same colour. Sensing that something was wrong, he looked back.

Getting surprised was not the nature of Clark. But the things he was seeing, he didn't want to believe it. The eyes of the sea dragon were vindictive. It was glowing red; his pupils were about the size of Clark's figure. Its massive tail, having the white scales, was arched like a rainbow and was continuously flickering. The sea monster had a way about him, a grace that was unmatched, as if got suddenly awake from a hibernation. It didn't have wings. Its sharp teeth, they appeared as if quenching for hunger. Its gigantic build starting from the face and slowing diminishing, ending at his tail, it was like the white dragon was preaching some kind of a toxic greed.

"Oh, you cruel sinner!" the dragon spoke, "What caused you to awake me? Don't you know that I have the flames residing inside my heart? I have been calm since fifty years. I'm a meditator. I'm the messiah. You have disturbed me. You have encouraged me. I can smell the impulse in you. My flames can burn you. You are a slender man. My fury is inconceivable and my omnipotent power is greater than any creatures you will meet. You cannot endure it. You cannot withstand it. My bite is venomous. All the fishes are my serpent. If I want, they can eat your flesh right now, chew you to bones. You better have a valid reason so that I can forgive you."

Clark could see inside the endless depth of his eyes a hidden wisdom. He wasn't afraid. He was just amazed to find such things in Oasis. His tone was frank against the revealing severity of the monster's hunger: "Fight me," spoke Clark.

Hearing it, the dragon's eyes became wide, and under the darkness of the water, they emerged with a red lamp-like colour. They were like sharp torch that Clark witnessed; the next thing was the creature's mouth, the sharp ray of the golden light under its throat, it made its way to swallow Clark. The next couple of minutes was dark for him. It was like he was breaking through some kind of a barrier. He tried speaking, but he couldn't speak. He tried to control his body, but he couldn't do that too. All around him, he could feel the liquid jelly. Against it, he couldn't react, or struggle, was also unable to think properly. He felt like his energy was draining. This went on for a couple of minutes. Then the strength of his body was coming back; it was like a single emotion that had its way to his consciousness and wasn't giving up. Soon, the faculty of his mind brought the rest of the energy, with control and judgement, reducing him to a plain sensation of seeing some shreds of light, as if a window was opening. Still, he couldn't see the whole frame properly. The liquidly touch that his body was feeling, it was going away, and his body was dropping. The shreds of light, it collectively came under a one frame under what appeared like a crevasse. Clark was going there. The tension of his nerves again was producing that kind of exhaustion inside his body as if he was being desperately kept awake of sleepless hours. The moment his body took a drop and hit the floor of a compact room, he thought that he was dead and the room was some kind of a heaven.

The compactness of the room made him wonder. His body had fallen beside a bed. He could see the white bedsheet on it, could grasp the touch of velvet. The cushions enveloped with the same. The bed had the reflection of a light on it, as if the shine of a moonlight. Clark tried to get up; the accumulated shock and strain had hit him bad. Though he felt like his strength was back, but his sudden emotions were conveying him a different meaning. As he tried to get up, he could see that the room was possessed with different steel lockers; they were joined with the walls. The ceiling had the depiction of the space shuttle's roof. If someone didn't have the experience of the space shuttle, that person could have conceived that ceiling like the design of some steel ladder's rung. But this was besides the point, right next to the bed, Clark's eyes laid on the standing figure against the hexagon glass. Outside the window, he could see the darkness of the universe, the stars twinkling; also, the curvature of some planet, whose reflection was falling on the bedsheet. The figure that stood in between the glass, she wore a summer top, exposing her back; on it, a shining circle—a socket for a plug. The length of her hair reaching her neck, Clark kept looking at her for a moment.

The image that his eyes were registering, they were providing him the feeling of disbelief. A weird thought made him think that he had to renounce his mind so that he could understand the mechanisms of his body. When the girl turned to look at him, he could see her heavy cheeks accompanied by dark eyebrows. Her grey eyes were like as though they were hiding some kind of a terror behind it. Her lips, her nose—it was the face of lost nonchalant. Clark could sense beneath the surface of her tightened expression a leader who had lost her way. The compact walls of the room had made her liveliness to vanish completely. When she saw Clark, a tear from her eyes dropped.

"You are inside the stomach of the dragon," she spoke, "you are inside the belly. Don't worry. The dragon is up made of a complicated structure. The artificial program in it is damaged and I'm trapped in it. I thought nobody would survive the bite of the dragon, but you did. Whenever the dragon chew somebody, I only got the leftover parts of that individual through the roof that you came in. But now you have come, I see hope. The universe and the planet that you can see behind me, is it just a wallpaper. This was where I came from, the planet of Vegavond. I was running as a president there. I knew that the opposition there was strong. I knew they had hidden the time travel emerald for me, but still, I ran for the president. I was giving the speech to my people…my last speech," her eyes rolled towards Clark, "I was telling the public how the opposition was flawed. How they were not concerned with the fulfilment of their desire, rather, they were only worried about their irrational feelings and their stomach. I was telling them how both irrational feelings and stomach were against the mind. I told them how humans cannot abandon the brain in the name of feelings and random beliefs. Some people were also fearful of the opposition because it was funded by Alfred Cox. He was planning to snatch the time travel emerald by fooling the opposition, but the opposition…my dad and his party, they also didn't know where time travel emerald was hidden. They were lying to Alfred. They all had to pay a price for it soon. The chances of me winning the election was quite high, so I got kidnapped by a mob, also funded by Alfred. They took me here, in the planet of Oasis. A man from the planet Zeda had programmed this dragon. This dragon is like my temporary body. I didn't know what the dragon was saying to you. I just know that whenever the dragon moves, it gives my body an energy—a life, but I'm forever bound by this place. Also, I cannot let Alfred steal the time travel emerald. You are my only hope. My father is dead. A random stranger is running my planet, wearing my father's mask. You have to do something. Do you even know what is it like to be bitter, resentful, and fearful? Do you even know what pain means? Once you understand this in yourself and how these emotions naturally come inside you, you will understand how these same emotions can occur in others. This is what I feel for my people."

"How old are you?" asked Clark.

"I'm seventeen."

"How come you are seventeen and running for the office?"

"The constitution of Vegavond was created by good people."

"I presume they are dead now," replied Clark.

"Why are you talking to me like this?" exclaimed the girl.

"I know that life is hard, but understand that you have to take harsh actions too. What is your name?"

"Cirri."

Clark had grasped the magnified parts of her life that she had uttered from her mouth. The voluntary evil that the people do to each other, it brings permanent and profound damage, that's what he felt about Alfred. He was bending and twisting people into their draconian forms who then voluntary becomes to work evil and the kind of bad things that they generate for themselves, it effects the whole universe as pain and suffering; Cirri was stuck in it—this was how Clark was looking at her. The cry for help from her to him was desperate. She told him about the wires that the room had, that it was there to charge her body. She also conveyed him that whenever she charges her body, she could not able to set the plug on her back for more than fifty seconds. "If you can hold the plug," she spoke, "for more than fifty seconds, then I think we can short-circuit the AI system of this dragon."

"You can die, Cirri," he spoke.

"I know, but we have to take this chance. Don't you wanna get out?"

"Yes, I do, but also, I wanna save you too."

Cirri could feel that Clark was the kind of man who wasn't relying on faith, or hope, rather, was the guy who relied on offering facts and proof. Coming inside the stomach of the dragon: Cirri's room, he indirectly proved her the qualifications of intelligence induced with the muscle power he had. She was naturally getting attraction to him, even if she was underage. This is his way, she said to herself, controlling the attributes of Clark's pleasing personality. As he came near her, she turned her back at him. Clark could see her lighted back circle, a root for the plug that he held in his hands. When the plug came near her back, it naturally got connected to her. To that, her eyes closed. The current pulsating around the plug reached her back. Clark could feel the shocks, but it did his rigid body nothing. Fifty seconds were about to get over and the hands of Clark, they were becoming black because his skin was burning. As the plug passed above the mark of fifty seconds, the current pulsation around the wires going to her body, the strong flashes had started to come out of it, hitting the room. To that, they got a strong jerk. Cirri told him that the dragon was in pain, the natural settings of the AI programme, they were experiencing something new. When Cirri started to shout, Clark hesitated, but she told him to keep going, to not lose the grip of his hands. His hands firm like his mind, they remained at the same position. He could see that the despair and pain reigned over Cirri, but something else had also started to take place: the room had begun to disappear and the wallpaper of the planet and the universe she had, instead of the wallpaper, the red eye of the dragon came in.

"It's him," Cirri shouted. "It's the eye of the AI programme. This eye always comes when it is in the mode to self-sabotage its system. "It's—" she couldn't complete her sentence. She had begun to shout at a continuous rhythm. The eye of the AI programme, watching them like they were some kind of bacteria—the wires around his eye like the cluster of arteries, everything had vanished suddenly. Now blackness beckoned them. Clark could feel the body of Cirri—same thing went for Cirri, but they both couldn't see each other's bodies. They both felt the return of liquid jelly around them, touching them. They couldn't speak. Their strength was ebbing away; also, their consciousness had started to fade. They felt like they were taking the sins of the whole mankind spreading among the different universes, then they felt that their bodies had lost the touch of gravity. After that they both felt like they were experiencing something—a shot, a feeling that they were accelerating upwards. Then they both saw a light, simultaneously, their consciousness was also returning back to them with their strength. The dragon had spit them out of the lake. Clark was first who got shot up tearing the crust, followed by Cirri. His body plunging just beside the shore along with her, he saw the dragon irrupting from the lake. His irruption was like a giant monster; his eyes red, his body scales white, the mountain behind him appeared like his playground. The ball of fire under its mouth was accumulating. It was aimed at Clark and Cirri. The moment the dragon spit the fury of fire, the moment Diana teleported in front of Clark and Cirri. From her hands, she created an electromagnetic shield. It stopped the fire reaching all three of them.

As the fire slowed down, now the dragon was the one who appeared to lose his consciousness. His last attempt of revolt didn't bring him anything, except his own death. To that, his body had completely shut off; it appeared to be swaying back and forth. It was just a matter of minutes that the dragon was about to take a massive drop. Diana was protruding out the shield from her hands; her artificial fingers had grown, current coming out from it, making the electromagnetic shield. Clark was watching that priceless possession of hers. He didn't know whether he had missed her, or longed for her, yet he deeply appreciated the gestures of her action. Her figure standing like of a leader, the lines of her back muscles and her hands lifting to control the shield, he was grasped by the authentic mannerisms that rendered him to just watch her. On the other hand, Cirri's consciousness hadn't come back. She lay beside him, beside the shore.

When the dragon's body hit the rest of the crust, the lake wasn't frozen anymore. The water rushed out from it in the form of a tide— low, but sharp, along with broken pieces of ice that were like bullets. The dome like shield covering them, it prohibited the hostility of the outside environment. The lake's water with the sharp ice shooting out of it had dismantled the shreds of islands around the lake. The pieces of ice that were left floating on the water, and on it, the broken body of the dragon—the inside, intricate wires of his system, electric sparks were coming out of it. Then the wisps of smoke surrounded its shattered body, resulting in the inevitable explosion. It shook rest of the trees around different islands that were left unaffected by this incident. When everything had started to calm down, Diana's shield had vanished. She turned and immediately looked at Clark.

"I'm sorry," she spoke. "I shouldn't have allowed you to dive."

"It's fine. I had already made that decision."

"What do you mean?"

"I was going to dive…with you, or without you," Clark replied.

She seemed to skip his emotions. Her eyes turning to Cirri, Diana could see that she was returning to life. As her eyes slowly opened, she was feeling, for the first time, a personal salvation to her; she could not name the purpose behind that salvation. She knew she was finally out of the sea dragon's belly, but she was determined that now she had to get out from the planet of Oasis. Feeling that, she looked at Clark.

"You have to steal the time travel emerald. You have to go to Vagavond with me. We have to save those people."

"You mean you need to save those people, and you need my help."

"That's correct," answered Cirri.

"But all of you need to first escape Oasis," interrupted Diana.

She is right, thought Clark. She was giving him that absolute expression which told him that he needed to first get inside the purple spire, to first steal the power of teleportation. Diana could see how Clark was giving his hand to Cirri so that she could get up. Diana could see the steps of her being depended on him. She observed. She felt strange, then Diana, as if suddenly contend with herself, started to walk. Clark and Cirri were behind her. The twilight shade of the evening had started to dim with the imminent night time. Diana knew that both their dresses were wet. She could see the cold engulfing Cirri the way in which she wrapped her arms around her, but Clark, if she knew him properly, and she did—now she did, would know that even if he was feeling cold, he wouldn't show it. This is his code, she thought, this is the sanction of his morality, she concluded. They all walked under the woods of the forest.

TWO TOUGH FATES MEETING

It was almost night. Diana felt alone even if she was walking with Clark and Cirri. A part of her emotion was telling her to teleport, but she couldn't do it. It wasn't the part of her nature: to abandon someone. On the other hand, she was hesitantly conscious of the woods. She has heard stories of the people residing in the different islands of Clinis, that they didn't like to be observed. In the back of her mind, another story had also started to touch her emotions, that how she used to come to her library at night sometimes, whenever her brother, Alfred, used to treat her bad, or whenever she had a fight with him, and he not approving her behaviour to suit the throne—these kinds of troubles always made her to run back to library. She never believed in the so-called throne. To counter the pretense that Oasis presented, she was building her library in the form of hut ever since she was a child. Alfred knew about it. Ever since he was a boy, he had given her sister, Diana, many wake-up speeches to live in accordance with the way the noble people lived in Oasis—she couldn't do that. She couldn't live with covering her whole body because it didn't have the level of enhancements others had. Instead, she relied on improving her soul, to delve in introspection and meditation, to bring that calm sense in her. It has always helped her; with it, she could feel the power of her teleportation, its grip: no fading and exhaustion, fast; also, she saw that too much enhancements did nothing to people; they didn't know how to operate their advanced system. Same went for Alfred, but still, he gave her speeches how reading didn't breed the right people.

The belligerent speeches with which he concealed the opinion of Diana's bookstore so that she could increase her knowledge, it didn't appeal to him. The perversity of it had changed the character of Alfred in Diana's mind since childhood, it was descended to fake masculinity minus the pragmatic part of his brain, which he didn't have at all. Though his educational background had made him throw some decent words during the important meetings regarding Oasis with Dark Storm, other than that he usually uttered nonsensical things. He always devalued her artistic integrity, never liked her library, now possessed by The Magician. When she thought about him, she looked at Clark. His faint smile at her was the suggestion of something important to her. She respected him, but deep inside, she had started to adore him; she just didn't want to identify those emotions. Cirri beside him, she could not condemn her, even if she wanted to—this emotion too, she didn't want to identify it. Instead, she just gazed at her, reflectively, and concluded that she walked like an injured kitten—agile, but delicate. The crudely way with which Diana's mind was operating, she called it fate, then she looked at the woods again. It reminded her about her library again and the horror behind it, which she had no words to describe.

Clark's body felt something looking at the preciousness of Diana's gait. He too didn't want to identify his emotions, that the spark that had rushed inside her body regarding Clark, he could feel the same inside him about her, like a loving frequency, but he didn't have the words for it. The structure of the reality they were in: the theme of the forest, and they marching forward ahead in order to find something, maybe a shelter, this was what Clark didn't want to rely on. He directly wanted to confront The Magician alone; a deep part of his mind also wanted to just leave Diana and Cirri, but he knew he couldn't. Like a leader, he had to be with them, like a team. Watching Cirri, she shivering with cold, the idea of shelter was inevitable. Their reliance on the footsteps of Diana, that she would find something, was also a different structure of the theme that produced the reality not in their favour. To that, Clark was having self-generated doubts. Walking with them, Clark was thinking that he was taking actions. The thought was so strong that its manifestation had started to take place: they all could hear something, a shout, but the place they were standing, they didn't really know whether it was a shout, or something else. But Clark assumed it that it was something important. He lifted Cirri and kept her on his back. Her legs were spread on the left and right side of his shoulders. Clark conveyed her to hold tight. Meanwhile, Diana had already started to run, following the heavy voice.

As they were running, the forest was fading into gaps that displayed in its vicinity a plain land which was greased with green, lush grasses. When the forest came to its end, they were behind a bush. Ahead of them, they could see an inn, the ceiling of it exhaling puffs of smoke. The sign of the inn on its door had the crescent moon, imitating the real shine of it, in a deep yellow colour. But also, ahead of the inn, they saw a family standing that appeared terrified out of their mind. Within their proximity—four, shabbily dressed men stood, exposing the enhancements of their body. Their exultant laughs coined them the term the natural thugs. One of them was holding an axe that was bigger than him. The guy also had a rough, long hair. He seemed to be the leader of the gang. He was constantly swinging the axe with both his hands; the yellow current that twirled around his arms also seemed to give an extra power to axe. It was aimed at a boy who stood in between the two windows of the inn, his back touching its brown wall. The window under the yellow lights of the inn constituted a large gathering of people; they were looking through the window. The silhouette of them also conveyed both Clark, Diana, and Cirri the expression that they too were terrified out of their mind.

The minute the leader of the gang swung the axe at the boy, his mother—separated from the gang, with her family witnessing this chaotic even, she dropped to her knees. It was at that moment too that Clark threw the Cirri from his back to Dianna and straight away ran with his maximum speed toward the boy. The boy didn't realize how Clark came at him before the axe. He just saw how Clark grip the axe with his left hand and the sheer power with which he threw the axe back at the leader of the gang, splitting his body in half, making the rest of the gang members to flee the scene with the intensity with which they first came at the inn. The boy watching Clark's bravery, he couldn't resist his new hero, he proceeded to hug him. The crowd inside the inn came out. They cheered for Clark.

When the mother of the boy came running at his son, in tears she hugged him, simultaneously, she acknowledged from her eyes the unpayable debt she owned to Clark. She could see the simplicity in which he wore his clothes, giving him the default expression of a person who preached justice, gained a splendor by living in the present moment. Watching his clothes wet, she asked him where he was coming from. He answered her that he was coming from the lake. To that, the crowd gathered around him gasped. They couldn't believe it. It brought out the murmurs from the crowd.

"Stop it!" spoke the boy's mother. "What happened to you?" she asked.

"Yes, what happened to you," came a random voice from the crowd, "there is a dragon living there. He used to kill our people. Even when the lake is frozen, he still finds a way to kill people."

"Well, you all don't have to worry about him from now. He is gone."

The crowd again gasped; they were looking at each other. "You killed him?" came another voice from them.

"No," said Clark. "I just found out that he is not living there anymore. You all don't have to worry."

Clark was fulfilling the crowd's desire in a way that they had not imagined would manifest in real life. When Diana, and on her back, Cirri, came—the crowd assumed that the man had a wife and a daughter. The boy's mother and beside her, his father, when they saw Clark's and Cirri's wet clothes, and Cirri about to catch the cold, they both offered the inn to them. The inn was a granite structure. Cirri was continuously looking at the sign above its door—a yellow crescent moon, as if it was real. She had the kind of face that carried neither approval nor resentment: her expressions had lost the attentiveness; like a paper, they were blank. The boy's mother, Martha, had guessed that the girl could get infected lungs, so she better prepares her a soup. Martha told the crowd that the facilities for her inn were done for the day and they all had to find some other inn if they want to have some enjoyable time. It seemed like nobody were in a mood. They were dispersing to their respected home. Meanwhile, the husband of Martha was looking at Diana's face with suspicion. He felt like he had seen Diana's face somewhere, but when she weirdly smiled back at him, killing his urgent desire of her real identity, this weird smile worked on him. He gave her another give that seemed to convey that he welcomed her.

Inside the inn, all three of them were eating the soup. Martha saw some peculiar, personal quality of Clark's smile, which was also a quality that she didn't saw in the noble people. It was in contrast to the impersonal, plain manner with which Diana ate her soup. She could read her thoughts. She could feel the way she was feeling about Clark, one minute thinking about The Magician, another minute, comparing Clark with him. The power of her telepathy had come with the sorcery chip that had been installed by her mother. That enhancement in her body gave her the power to read thoughts of those people who had installed a matching enhancement software as of hers. Martha could get the calm nature of Diana. Even when she conversed with her, she saw that her voice was eloquent. The sorcery chip that had been installed in her was like an additional utility patch: it was limited; it wasn't constructed anymore. Her mother gave it to her when she was small, put it in the plug which was on the right side of her shoulder, which Martha also made sure to cover it up with a shawl. The only limitation of her chip was that she couldn't read the thoughts of people whenever she was hit with anxiety and she was struck by it not so long ago. She thought that she caught Diana at the right moment. When she turned the direction of her head at Cirri, she couldn't read her, or Clark, as she proceeded to move her gaze at him.

Under the stillness of the inn, she enjoyed the movements of her guests, that they were enjoying her hospitality. She saw her son, Alex, on the other side of the sofa, laughing with Clark, his hero possessing a natural, superlative gesture but talking as though a friendly neighbourhood guy. She had given her husband's clothes to Clark. It had fitted him tight, exposing the strength of his muscles; whereas, Cirri, she had given her his son's clothes, a sweater accompanied by the trousers. And as far as Diana went, Martha was glancing at her. She could read her thoughts. She could feel the intensity with which she looked at Clark, while her husband and him were having a conversation. Diana eyes were not at his body, but at his face, as if she was witnessing his soul and how it was innocently natural. She saw his head turned at her husband and whenever Clark cracked a joke, the corners of her mouth made a full circle smile.

And whenever Clark looked back at her, she saw him, as if welcomed his soul, in an open, joyous, and friendly manner. Then Martha deeply observing her, making her way to read her thoughts, she noticed that Diana was asking herself why she was feeling alone, and now, all of a sudden, why that loneliness had vanished—Diana could not answer. She was telling herself that her mind had stopped working, that it was encountering something pure in Clark, something spiritual. Then she concluded that many girls would fall for a man like him and would only see his outside appearance, but she, in her existence, she would always see his soul, so that it could dwell on that spiritual connection. Listening and feeling her, Martha's left eye dropped a tear. Clark immediately caught her and asked her about her wellbeing. She answered him that it was the tear of joy, that she was enjoying the art of conversation in this gathering.

Like an audience, Martha was watching all of them. On her shoulder, Alex had come and had fallen asleep. Then she saw something on the window that had made her abandon her sound. Her voice started to trail off, then she immediately closed her eyes as if she was abandoning the faculty of her sight. She was convincing herself with reasons that what she was saw on the window was not real—an enlarged eye of a beast, observing the harmony inside the room, preparing it to dismantle it. The cruel flicker of lights inside her inn reduced her into a state of terror. Then she shouted as the eye again reflected on the window; she couldn't bear it no more. Clark got alert; he took Alex and put it on the sofa. He felt a lost sense of time. Then he understood the sudden shout of Martha when the ceiling of the inn started to tear off, exposing the frigid night. Watching the hands of the beast, the bulging shoulders covered with an armour plate, back having the steel wings, legs bulged too with the same kind of armour plate attached to it, and his head a vicious, typical depiction of a beast's face—Clark knew that he had finally met The Magician.

He run towards him, while telling with an almost calm tone to Diana to take care of the family and Cirri. But as he tried to climb The Magician's giant legs, the current emanating from it shot Clark a few feet away. Though he came back with the brutal hand shots, making deep dents inside his legs, also, resisting the current, but he could see the right hand of The Magian's, that it had gripped Martha. He could hear her chronic shouts and the agonizing pain which with the beast held her. Clark, not able to resist this, he again tried to climb him. As he made his way up the body, the current that the beast naturally sparked, its voltage had become malicious. He felt like his was body was losing strength again, but also, he couldn't watch the demise of Martha. In an instant, The Magician had become his deadliest enemy. When he reached his top back, The Magian flapped his wings. He took off to the sky carrying Martha under his hand and Clark on his back. Clark was continuously hitting him with the tight blows with both his hands, as if installing with each blow enlightenment into him, but The Magician was the man of cruel violence. He was over the lake of Clinis when he sacrificed Martha; it was due to the blows that Clark unleashed on his back, breaking the evolved circuitry there. But as Martha was falling down, Clark jumped from his back. He could see the hand of Martha—a sign of help, pointed at him in the mid-air, but as Clark was in the air, The Magician also took an inverted dive. He caught Clark with his hands, while Martha, she had lost the hope. There was no one to save, then out of nowhere, Diana teleported beside her in the mid-air. She could see that Martha was about to hit the floated ice on the lake—the previous chaos produced by the sea dragon. She was trying to teleport Martha along with her, but as The Magician was close to her, she couldn't able to do it. Diana had started to fall too. Clark was witnessing this; to that, he continued with his punches. He was hitting the area around his index finger and thump that had clasped him close. Trying to accumulate his full strength, even though he knew his strength was ebbing away, he hit him as if he was seeking redemption against his sin. It made The Magician to change his direction. He flew again toward the sky.

As they both, Martha and Diana, were about to hit the thick ice sheet on the lake, Diana immediately used her power of teleportation successfully. She took Martha with her under the nearby woods with her family. Meanwhile, Clark was up in the sky with The Magician. He could see that his punches had started to prove ineffective. As the beast was squeezing him tight, his strength was dropping drastically. Suddenly, he could see his wings flapping slowly under the drifting clouds of Oasis. Clark was fading as The Magician eyes were accumulating a laser beam. Clark knew that he was about to suffer the pinnacle of his power. He knew he was about to encounter the vicious kind of malevolence he had. He questioned what kind of structure operated inside of him that made The Magician a unique kind. When the beam hit Clark's body, to The Magician, Clark had seemed to lose his soul. His last move was to fiercely charge the body of Clark carried by his fist to one of the islands of Clinis so that he could completely tear his body to pieces; it was also a proper kind of burial by The Magician.

When the giant structure of his body was coming to the ground, Clark's body was charging with the beam. Instead of damaging him, Clark's body had already developed a way to counter his beams— the most ferocious one was when he encountered the beams of Dark Storm in New York, after spending his time in a capsule, his body was accustomed to the deepest levels of beams. His body soaking the beams of The Magician, for a moment, had appeared to be shut, but now, the cells of his body had recharged him fully. It had brought back his strength despite the electric shocks that the beast's body automatically emitted. Now, Clark was the one who unleashed a powerful beam of light from his eyes that tear the bottom left of The Magician's torso. Clark could see the weird liquid coming out from it. As the blue sunrise made its presence known, The magician's body was crashing like a spaceship, carrying the trails of smoke with it. It crashed against the one of the islands of Clinis, obliterating its forest, while also making a huge dent inside the lake. The dent was caused by the beast's falling leg—it was the point of contact, then the body of his dragged few kilo meters away completing the island. The dent was so deep and huge that all the water of the lake had made its way inside it. The lake looked like as if it had suffered from a drought. The hole also swallowed the remaining big ice sheets on it. If The Magician was like darkness, Clark was like light. Darkness couldn't stand against light. It has to be wiped out of existence. Clark's body was pristine; it was pure light. It was successful in eliminating the dark. The intersection of the two tough fates met with a new order.

THE ULTIMATUM

Clark was still in The Magician's hand, but the grip of his hand had loosened up and it had break him free. If one could see him, he would appear dead, but he wasn't. Some fingers of his hands were twitching, the movements of it were very negligible, but Clark could notice The Magician's defiance to not give up. His bottom left torso had been half-split from the beams of Clark's eyes, but Clark, he could see his immaculate struggle. The gigantic body of his had settled its position against the mountain, situated at the end of the island. The Magician's back upended, Clark saw that in the middle of his lower back a box was there. It was installed inside him. Its continuous beeps were like the last breaths. Clark didn't want The Magician to suffer no more, so he proceeded to take that box out. When he did, he saw that the beast's body had started to shrink, and the box that he took out from his body and was now in his hands, it had burst out into a weird jelly, a bacteria, that had its own life. The jelly was fierce on his hands; it tried to snatch his face, but Clark again fired the beams from his eyes to kill the bacteria. When he looked at The Magician, he saw a new life in him. His body was normal. The muscles on his body had shrieked too. The metal wires on his head made him itchy. He was limping and coming towards Clark like a normal person.

"Thank you," he spoke when he came near him, "you killed that bacteria that was inside me…for god knows how many years. Thank you."

He turned to go, then The Magician halted. He again looked back at Clark. "Oh, and one more thing. Alfred is waiting for you. The member of the gang that you had destroyed in one of the islands of Clinis, the rest of the group had reported the incident to Alfred. They were his people. If you are going his way, be careful, he has an army waiting for you. Go get that power of teleportation so that you can get out of this planet."

"What about you? Don't you wanna defeat him?"

"I'm not your ally, Clark. My first priority is to visit the home of those people whom I killed in an unapologetic manner. Now, I'm going to their family members to apologize for my actions. I know that they won't accept my apology, but I have to try."

He began his walk, and in matter of minutes, he disappeared while going toward the forest. In front of Clark stood a lane that was a brutally dismantled deforestrated area. On his left and right were the stretched, parted trees. It was the result of The Magician's body that had come from the sky and had been crashed there. On the other hand, Clark had to begin his running, so he did. On the lane, his pace met with a lot of big rubbles of wood. When he crossed the lake, he saw different fishes, their bodies made out of a metal in a plea to inhale air. Clark felt like he had sacrificed them; this feeling made him to feel bad. As he made his way to another island of Clinis where Diana and Martha's family were waiting for him, he returned to them as if everything was okay. But in his mind, he knew that it wasn't. He had a war waiting for him and all he had was Diana. He thought that this was how the moral code of the outer world worked. But then he looked at Diana, he felt an intense light-heartedness. He again thought that if she was with him, then he had to not wait anymore. He felt like whatever the decision he would take, as long as Diana was with him, every battle was easy; wherever there was uncertainty, she would make him feel that there were no conflicts. Martha couldn't read him, but she could diffidently read Diana's expression and her heart. Martha saw that Diana was nervous about him, at the same time, was proud. They all were under the bright daylight of the wood. When they started walking toward the inn, Clark didn't tell them that what went under him about the army of Alfred. As far as what he knew, he was just planning that he has to be subtle in his way to get out of the inn without informing anybody. Cirri was getting along with Alex. Martha's husband was talking to Diana. Martha and Clark were behind them. As they walked, Martha handed him her sorcery chip. Clark, when he had a closer look, didn't know what Martha presented to him. He even told her that he didn't have any plugs. But Martha held her hand. She cut his wrist; it was like a scratch that made his blood to seep out a bit. The moment the minute chip touched his blood, the chip was inside him. Slowly, the scratch got disappeared. He felt possessed with something, but he didn't know what. Martha conveyed him that soon he would be aware of the power that she gave him for saving her life and her family, the power of telepathy.

Reaching the inn, a large gathering of people was waiting for Clark. The stories of his bravery had been well enveloped into the minds of the people and now they wanted to see him. The inn was shattered, but the people didn't care. They surrounded him, so did all the members that he had with him: Diana, Cirri, and the inn's owner. Martha had made the inn's most famous drink, a heartthrob gin, for all of them. She indirectly conveyed Clark to not drink it. After fifteen minutes of drinking that gin, all the people around Clark had fallen asleep. Only Martha and Alex were standing on their feet, but her gaze paused at Alex, after five seconds, he had also fallen on the ground because he had acquired the taste of the gin, stealthily. Then Martha looked at Clark.

"You can go now," she said.

Clark understood what went inside her heart. Without saying anything, he ran. He crossed the islands of Clinis. As he made his run, Alfred's end had become his fulfilment; without it, he wasn't complete, or would feel complete. He had reached the mountains where the beam of first tri-pod like machines that he encountered near the bazaar had shot itself due to his interference, cutting the fragments of the mountain. And now, he was at the end of it. A new type of jungle was unravelling before him. It was the jungle where The Magician used to stay, but now, there was no magician. The whole jungle was open to him. His pace was accelerating like a speed of a local jet, but he immediately stopped. He felt that someone was following him. He turned, but found no one standing behind him. The sorcery chip that Martha had given Clark, it made him to feel the presence of Diana.

"You are here! I know!" he said.

Clark heard the rustles behind the bushes, and then, like a clean, pure air, he saw Diana coming out of it. Her figure stood tall. Her face had become pink catching up the pace of Clark. The sun had not vanished and the sky was deceptively orangish and blue. Clark knew immediately what she felt about him, could read her thoughts, could sense her urgency, and could interpret her need to be with him. "You thought that I drank that gin?" she asked and continued her talk: "You know that you can't leave us... What about Cirri? ...Don't you wanna go to Vagavond?" she wasn't stopping and Clark was coming at her. She couldn't get the expression of his face, while she talked. He just was coming straight, then when he reached, he took her back by his arm, and kissed her.

"I feel the same," he said. She didn't say anything. She was just embracing the ignition inside her body caused by Clark's kiss; also, the sensation of his arm grabbing her back. Her head was closer to Clark. She heard his voice inside her mind.

"Is it weird that I just heard your voice in my mind?" she asked.

"You are right." –he didn't say these words from his mouth; he was conversing with her through telepathy. Even though she knew she would fight the battle with him to defeat his brother, Alfred, but when Clark kissed her, she didn't feel any fear, just excitement. It was like her world had fallen apart, but in a good way. Now, they both were running toward the castle of Alfred. As they were close to finish the forest, Diana saw her library, but Clark's mind said to her that it was okay, some things had to be left alone. She heard him in her mind and she accepted what he was trying to convey. They were paused for a minute, then they left the forest. As they reached the garden near the bazaar, ahead of it the castle of Alfred, along with it more castles, on the waterfall—everything had disappeared. The grandstand of army was in the air. Alfred's castle was also in the air. It was like a dome and around it had four pillars, all white and he probably staying in it. The dome, above it, had the purple spire. Clark had to get there, but the army—robotic balls flying in the air, their face having the three sharp legs like a nail—they were in thousands. From each single yellow ball, like a model of some artillery, a wire protrude from it. It was attached to the helmets of those people who were controlling those yellow balls. They were flying too. As soon as they saw Clark, they started firing their missiles at him. He was dodging it perfectly.

Meanwhile, Diana had teleported herself to the dome. She could see that Alfred had attached himself to the throne, behind it the portal of teleportation. He remained seated. His eyes were all purple. On his head, he was wearing some kind of a cap, a broad thread that was enveloped around it. He had done everything to topple the coming fury of Clark; the only weird thing was that there was no trace of Dark Storm's people helping him in this quest. She was speaking to him, but he wasn't answering her. His figure was like a statue, soaking something, not of this world, but as if an energy from another dimension from the portal behind him. Diana kept on telling him to do something, to not get involved in this fight. She told him that he had to change his regime, to cure his people, and to unthread the constant wintery weather. She wanted him to understand the natural beauty of Oasis, that that natural beauty came from the people of Oasis, noble or regular, it didn't matter as long as people believed in love. Alfred was not answering. He was still soaking in some kind of an energy, but as Diana came near at him, his purple eyes fiercely turned at her. He raised his left hand and through it, a purple light imitating a shape of a rope came and lifted Diana a few feet above the ground. The purple rope was strangling her. She tried to teleport herself, but she couldn't able to do it. Alfred was laughing boastfully, and Clark could hear what went inside Diana's heart and brain. He could hear her heartbeats dropping down slowly.

In the fight with the mechanic balls, he had managed to clung on the wire of one of it, destroying the person who carried that ball. Manipulating the ball by removing its middle leg, he had marched himself to the other balls hovering right in front of him. They had started to shoot him and his carriage, but he immediately left the machine that he was on, jumping continuously to another machine, then another, and then another to reach the hovering castle. In this process, Clark had managed to remove half the mechanic balls. As soon as he landed with a roll up on the marble of the castle, the mechanic balls that were left, followed him. They landed themselves into intricate machines, having the arms and legs of a robot. The people of Alfred were sitting under the stance where the robot's faces should be there. They were protected by a glass, and with them, they were having the gears of the robots from which they had planned to destroy Clark. When one of the robots charged at Clark with its mechanic run, the robot proceeded with the left hood. Clark dodged it and punched his glass instead. He killed the person inside it too; hence, the robot. It made rest of the robots at once to charge at him. To that, Clark dispatched the hands of the already obliterated robot beside him. He took the arms and flung the left arm toward the incoming robot and the right to the robot who was behind the robot he charged. He did it for few minutes until all the robots were down. The people whose robots were dead but were not killed, yet was injured, they fled the scene by jumping from the hovering castle and diving below the river of the garden.

When Clark entered the dome by destroying the gates of it, he saw Diana, her hands trying to untangle the grip of the purple rope that was coming through the hand of Alfred. Clark, furious, he came running at Alfred. The moment he punched him, it did nothing to Alfred. Diana was desperate to inhale the air and Clark was desperate to end Alfred's life, but he could read Diana inside his mind, that she was telling him to be calm to evoke his real power. To that, Clark was deeply inhaling and breathing so that he could align his breath, energy, and body work. It was hard, but it was necessary. The right hand of Alfred had gripped his neck. His hands that were throwing the jabs at him had become infective, but Diana struggling and almost in a position to faint, Clark finally unleashed the laser beams from his eyes. He was able to cut the purple rope that was knotted to Diana, but he couldn't do anything about the next move. He turned his laser beams at Alfred, but it didn't do anything to him. Clark's face was becoming purple because the blood was not going to his brain, and Diana, who fell on the ground, her strength was gone. Her body was dragging. She was still looking for answers to defeat Alfred, then she saw his throne, that it too was emanating a purple colour. Seeing that, she dragged her body there. She could see that Alfred's attention was only on Clark, to choke him to death. She could see that he was desperate. In between the throne, Diana saw a small dagger. She also could see that it was sparkling with the purple colour. When she took it, the purpleness of the dagger had remained. With that, she stabbed Alfred. He didn't know when the dagger came inside his body. His purple eyes—the source of his power, was gone. He even tried to teleport himself, but he couldn't do it. The portal behind his throne had started to collapse. Clark, without saying anything to Diana, or using the power of his telepathy, he made his way to jump inside the portal.

When he jumped, he was in a weird wormhole. The tunnel was sparkling with all sorts of colours as if he was on the way to discovery the mystery of the universe. With the tunnel, he had reached a supersonic speed. He didn't know how and when he landed inside a hall room. The hall was supported by huge rectangular columns that were tilted, giving the support to the rest of the hall that he couldn't see. Clark only saw the red lights amalgamating with the darkness of the hall. The rectangular columns, outside of it was another universe. He could see planets and different stars. Then out of nowhere two gigantic figures appeared in front of him. Their whole body was white and was covered with a maroon shawl. They wanted to meet Clark. They introduced him as the guardians. They told him that the portal of teleportation that they had created was not carried by the worthy people, until now. They congratulated him. They told him that Clark now possessed the power of teleportation. They told him that he could travel to any planets now, could enter any universes, or galaxies. They told him to just use his power of teleportation because they were done talking. Clark, when he used his power of teleportation, he teleported to the planet of Oasis. He attended to the state of Diana. When he reached there, he saw that she was with Dr. Hamilton, could also see Cirri, going inside his spaceship that he carried when he came from Earth. Dr. Hamilton conveyed him that he missed him and he also told him that the government of Earth, the secret service people, had seen him fight. To that, they want to give back his spaceship. With Dr. Hamilton, Cirri, and Diana—Clark was back in his spaceship. He came alone in the planet of Oasis, now, he was leaving with a new family. Their next destination was set to Vagavond to steal the time travel emerald.

CONCLUSION

Thank you again for buying this book!

I hope this book was a pleasure for you to read.

Thank you and good luck!

CPSIA information can be obtained
at www.ICGtesting.com
Printed in the USA
LVHW020356301120
672964LV00031B/1696